Blissful Ignorance

Vol 1

Jaylen Wilson

NoHoodPublishing

CONTENTS

PRELUDE

I leisurely strolled down an aisle of beverage filled refrigerators to my left, and an array of snacks, all shapes and sizes, to the right. Within the last door to the left were multiple single-file rows of milk placed on four shelves, one atop the other. I obliviously grabbed a carton from the top shelf, middle row, failing to even check its expiration date. There wasn't much of anything to eat back at home, and I wasn't particularly in the mood to go full-on food shopping, so this miniscule bodega just up the street from my house was the next best thing. I scanned the shelves to my right before pulling the only decent-looking box of cereal from the bunch. This would have to do for now. Approaching the lineless counter toward the entrance of the establishment, I saw my older brother, Jabari, whom most opted to call Bari, awkwardly scanning his surroundings. The two of us had always mimicked our dad by allowing curl-sprouting follicles to produce semi-condensed woolliness atop our heads. Nevertheless, a few years back, Bari chose to have our good friend Ivanna section his afro off into numerous quadrants, each containing a braid of its own. To compliment this coiffure, shortly after, he allowed the flattened stubble upon his face to swell slightly, producing a well-developed yet kinky landscape of hair. I couldn't be bothered to make any such transition from the thicket of hair, north of my brow. Favoring a more subtle demonstration of manliness than Bari, I snipped down the prickly blanket of hair enveloping my face, leaving only a remnant hanging stiffly from my chin. In spite of differing preferences, both facial and cranial, we couldn't help sharing the world's most widespread eye pigment. Our skin complexions weren't far off from one another either, as mine was just a tad less umber than Bari's. Additionally, the bridge of my nose was quite broad in comparison to his while, in the case of nasal apex's, I was bested. For fear of having his stomach return to its protruding form of time past, Bari dedicated himself to exercise, working on his core along with well-sculpted muscles which were far more imposing than my own. I'd managed to drag him out of the house to come along with me. He gave off a shudder as the chill which had followed us into the store crept up his exposed legs. But I found it hard to sympathize with him given it had been weeks since the last remotely warm day yet, here he was, wearing unironed shorts, a t-shirt, and sandals with socks.

"Hey, Naaji," said Andrea, the buttery-faced cashier with a smile. Her straightened blonde hair was in an unusual ponytail today.

"What's up?" I asked, placing our two items on the transparent counter.

"Work," she dryly replied while retrieving bags for the cereal and milk. Given the fact that conversations between Andrea and I consisted solely of ice-breaking small talk, it was no surprise that this exchange came to an abrupt end. Though he didn't show it, Bari was ecstatic. He had to be since the eerie silence enveloping the store meant his time out of the house wouldn't be extended any longer than it needed to be by chit chat. Traffic whizzing by outside thankfully began to fill the quietude until she told me the price of the purchase. I then unveiled my satisfyingly leathery wallet, and fished out a ten dollar bill from within. Andrea opened the register and began fiddling with money on her side of the counter. "Change," she said, holding a few dollars in her left hand, and a fist of coins in the other. Hands cupped, I met her halfway, before dumping it all in my pocket.

Before grabbing our bags, I thanked her, though they seemed more flimsy than reliable which forced me to hold the carton of milk by its handle through the bag, contrary to the cereal bag that I handled normally.

"Sure," Andrea grinned.

Bari darted out the door. "Hold up!" I cried, following after him.

"What? It's time to go home."

Bari was scarred- doomed to never be who he once was. Ever since our parents were stolen from us en route from a typical business trip, he'd practically converted to a shut-in, and was always on edge to say the least. Confronting him about it wasn't much of an option because he'd just get defensive, and a full-blown argument over what was best for him would commence. It'd reached the point that something as trivial as convincing him to accompany me up our own street felt like I'd won the lottery.

I nudged Bari as we turned the corner. "You wanna pick something up for dinner later?"

"Nah, I'm having cereal."

Typically, whenever mom and dad went on one of their trips, my brother and I would always make plans of our own, spending far more time away than at home until they returned. But those days were clearly on the back burner.

"Come on, it'll be-"

"No!" snapped Bari. "Why can't we just hang out at home?!"

The one upside to Bari's condition was that although he preferred not to leave the house, being separated from me was something he avoided just as much, allowing for opportunities like this run to the bodega.

"I'm worried about you, bro."

"I'm good. Just drop it."

"At least think about coming back out," I pleaded.

"Fine," replied Bari. I doubt he means it, but pray he *does*. After passing a few more houses, we step up onto our rickety front porch that cries out with each step taken on it. There wasn't much to it besides a wooden base, railings, and a few plastic seats to sit on which we anchored to the deck with chains leading to bricks beneath. Bari's keys danced in his hand before he wiggled the house-designated one into the front door, leading me in. I barely closed and locked the door behind myself when Bari scrambled upstairs. Taking a seat on our two-part beige couch, I sighed and looked around the spacious room. It had progressively become the loneliest part of the house as our dad accumulated more fame and success than any of us could have imagined. Now it was little more than a grim reminder of what used to be, equipped with a huge flat screen TV, practically spanning the entire wall it hung from, artsy paintings galore, a carpet with well-blended colors, and a door frame where the TV ended, granting entrance to our kitchen.

I then realized that I, unconsciously, still held the two bags in my hands, prompting me to rise and trot into the kitchen where I placed the carton of milk in our barren refrigerator, and the cereal in the adjacent overhead cabinet. In hindsight, our diamond-studded dinner table which sat dead center in the kitchen was a huge waste of money. We never really had any guest come over to be impressed by it, and hardly ever ate dinner as a family with our late parents anyway.

I poked my head out to the living room. "Bari!"

"What?" I heard him faintly reply from the floor above.

I had no real reason in particular for calling him. "Uh, whatcha doing!?"

"Relaxing! Why!?"

No legitimate reason for my outburst came to mind. "Nothing! Nevermind!"

I listened hard for a response while passing the staircase to put my shoes in their place below our coat rack, but nothing came.

"Aye, what time's your date!?" he finally replied.

I'd completely forgotten that Ivanna and I had plans to meet up for lunch. "Huh!?" I asked. "It's not a date!"

"What time you going!?"

"Right now! Gonna meet her at Vern's!"

"Be careful!" said Bari.

I slid back into my shoes. "Gotchu! See ya later!" I shouted before grabbing my car keys from the diminutive table to the doors right. The chilly outdoors now whistled with more constant and sharp fangs of air chomping into my skin.

Our all black SUV sat alongside mom and dad's chrome, luxury car in the driveway to the left of the steps. We were well off enough to each have our own vehicle, but we made a partnership out of everything else, so this was no different. The frigid driver-side door bit into my palm as I opened it, and leapt into the even less welcoming, ice-cold seat. A rich scent of pine cone, lining the car, was its only saving grace. I gently pressed on the start button with my thumb, and placed our car keys in the center console cup holders. She hummed with satisfaction. Once the gear was shifted into reverse from park, the screen betwixt both seats displayed the area behind me. Even with this added advantage, my backing up and parking were, without a doubt, my kryptonite. I quickly scanned my surroundings, let two cars pass, then eased my foot off the brake. Our vehicle rolled on its own backwards out of the driveway, into the street while I gently spun the wheel left, then right, shifted to drive, and proceeded down my street. As always, I unconsciously switched my foot over to the brake just in time to avoid tumbling over a formidable speed bump.

Our home was in prime position, practically at the border between up and downtown, granting close access to either end of the spectrum. The diner was a few blocks uptown, and being that I was already running late, I increased my speed, knowing the traffic light at my corner would soon glow red. This was an empty effort, however, as my entrance to the intersection was halted, commencing the turn of the others. Vehicles of all shapes, sizes, and colors came from both directions. I was quite accustomed to the heavy afternoon traffic of Jersey City, especially on a main street like the one I sought entrance to. Pedestrians-mostly students on their way home from school- practically rubbed against the nose of my vehicle as they crossed the street in front of me. It wasn't like I could blame them though. The length of my SUVs hood covered a chunk of the crosswalk. The red light abruptly gave way to green, but I allowed one more kid to cross, and squinted to examine my surroundings before making a right turn. I found myself sandwiched between parked cars to my right and other cars advancing forward to my left. All the vehicles moved together like a school of fish, refusing to be left behind at a red light. Once I reached the diner a few blocks down, two nearby cars had a large gap between them, allowing my entry into its half-empty parking lot, left of the brick building. I reached down to unbuckle my seatbelt, only to realize I'd never put it on to begin with, and exited the vehicle, double tapping the lock button on my car keys after throwing the door shut. The few cars within the lot, one of which being Ivanna's dad's emerald van, were no indication of the diners great popularity and success since opening years prior to the births of Bari and I. They served great food, but it was admittedly a bit overrated, especially by our parents who seemed to eat there every chance they got, both as a couple, as well as with Bari and I. Stepping around the corner, *Vern's Diner,* lit up in bold lettering for all to see, greeted me above the four steps to reach the front door. I trotted up the stairs, opened the door, checked for anyone behind me, and let it close as I entered. Seeing only a handful of booths occupied came as no surprise. At the podium near the entrance stood a friendly looking woman, with a stack of menus. "Good afternoon, sir!" she said. Table for one?"

"Somebody's waiting for me," I smiled.

She turned her head back to scan the few heads peeking over the lines of booths. "Is it a young lady?"

"Yeah."

"That her?" asked the woman, leaning toward me and pointing.

I saw the upper half of Ivanna's head. "Yeah, that's her."

"Perfect! I left your menu over on the table."

I thanked the hostess, and speed-walked over there. Our booth was in the middle of the three aisles. A couple sat adjacent to ours. Ivanna looked great as always. She possessed eyes with a mocha pigmentation, making them far more unique than my own as well as dark yet radiant skin on which glimmers of light loved to dance about. She had oil-glistened curls which, to my bewilderment, were flowing freely in an almost messy manner halfway down her back, contrary to their usual form as an orderly bun, yet they still managed to be complementary to the overall look. Her eyebrows neatly hovered above her eyes and though she has a semi-thin nose, it could still be considered nubian. Below it lied her naturally full lips.

"My bad," I quickly told Ivanna. "I forgot we were coming here." She sprung to her feet and I received her usual affectionate hug.

"It's cool. I just got here a little bit ago." Before she sat back down, I saw she had on sweatpants, slippers meant for the outdoors, and a considerably thick jacket regardless of the warm flow of air inside.

"How are you guys doing today?!" asked an unfamiliar voice, startling me. The voice's owner revealed herself. "I'm Tina," she said, smiling ear to ear. Her hair was cut to a buzz, and she actually pulled it off well. Her checkerboard apron flowed down just past her knees, and she had a tiny notepad and pencil handy. "I'll be your waitress this afternoon! Can I start you off with any drinks?"

"Sure," I swiftly replied, "I'll take a water with two lemons."

"Alright," said Tina. "What'll you be having, miss?"

she asked, turning to Ivanna.

Ivanna replied, "Raspberry lemonade please" whilst sporting a cordial smile.

"Comin' right up," said Tina with a blinding one, as if in contest. The pop song being played drowned out any conversations from other tables to mere murmurs.

"So ugh-"

Tina was back with our drinks. "Here ya go guys," she said placing the beverages on the table. "Water with two lemons and a raspberry lemonade! Have you guys had a chance to look at your menus yet?" Ivanna and I nodded no in unison.

"But I know what I'm getting already," I told her. "How 'bout you, Ivanna?"

"Um, sure."

"What'll it be?" asked Tina.

"Baby-back ribs," I replied while Ivanna subtly frowned

Tina scribbled away on her notepad. "Would you like a full or half rack?"

"Half rack."

"Uh huh, would you like any sides with that?"

"No thanks," I said softly.

Tina turned to face Ivanna. "And what would *you* like today, ma'am?"

Ivanna replied, "I'll take a cheeseburger with fries."

"Will that be all?"

We both nodded.

"Alrighty, you're all set. I'll be back with your meal shortly."

My mom and dad loved spending time with us as a family, but they easily spent far more of their minimal free time going on dates. Their relationship showed no signs of faltering. They always held hands. They always laughed together. They always made up after disagreements. They always compromised. It was great to witness, and I hoped for even a fraction of the same when the time was right.

After about fifteen minutes, Tina returned with our meals. "Here you guys go," she said, hastily placing the plates holding our respective dishes in front of us, causing the least noisy clank of metal on wood she could. I striped the bones of their barbecue sauce slathered meat and placed them neatly in the huge crater of space on my plate that lacked any sides dishes. After my first gigantic bite into a slab, I looked over at Ivanna's slow, methodical approach to consuming her food in which she, for some reason I could not comprehend, used her fork and knife to cut her already somewhat miniature burger into sections, picking up each one by poking the fork through it.

"The hell are you doing?" I asked, chuckling at her.

"Keeping my hands clean," she smiled back.

This was a good time with a good friend. But life was too balanced for the good to continue for long. It was only a matter of time.

CHAPTER 1:
PLEASURES MINE

Noise from all sorts of devices rang through the tunnel, resembling that of a train, as a yellow hoopty, covered in foamy soap, rolled in front of me from Cole's station. I trained the more powerful of two nearby hoses on the vehicle, not even considering the pressure could realistically dent it even further. Upon flipping its switch, water came bursting from the nozzle and blew soap along with griminess away. I put a slight bend on my knees as to not lose control and slowly adjusted the hoses aim until leaving the entire passenger side spotless. Once everything else was blasted clean of soap and bird droppings, I gave the ok for Julius, the track operator upstairs, to send this hoopty to Lamar on drying duty. Honestly, with all the advanced technology at his disposal, our boss could very well have fired us all with no dropoff in production. But still, he looked out for his fellow man, even granting us layed back dress code plus station rotation to minimize monotony. Shelly's Hyper Wash was made up of the tunnel I stood in, a waiting area, viewable through square glass directly behind me, and Shelly's office. Lighting came from the tunnels entrance and exit as well as inside where our customers were given a view of their cars journey via flat screens. I looked at a clock near our entryway inside and realized my shift had reached its end before yelling, "Yo, I'm out!" to the others.

"Peace!" shouted Cole, one fist in the arm.

"Catch you later!" called Lamar from his station as I went inside. My coworker, Neil was sitting amongst a few guests but stood up and shook my hand upon seeing me. He'd come to work, comfy as usual, sporting a sweatsuit.

"What's up, Naaj'?"

"Just grabbing my check and going home," I said. "You?"

"Same old," he replied, walking out to take my spot. His hair had an almost super-human glow to it no matter what angle one chose to view it from.

"Naaji," someone suddenly called.

"Huh?" I turned only to see my boss, leaning out of his office, dress shirt and polka-dot tie partially exposed.

"You got a second?" he asked.

"Yeah, I was just coming to see you."

The moment I entered his office, I was met with a firm handshake before he welcomed me to sit. This space had to be the most humble I'd ever seen for a owner of an establishment. Riddled with cardboard boxes and no windows, the main attraction was his desk, sitting between us, full of papers plus a few picture frames. He gently messaged his outstretched beard in silence which more than compensated for him having a hairless head.

"I won't keep you long," he said, "I just wanted to let you know you've been doing great."

"Thanks," I blushed.

"Well keep it up, and you'll be getting a raise real soon."

Just a few weeks in and I was already being considered for a raise that I didn't even want. In fact, lower wages would have been fine by me had Shelly allowed it.

"Oh, no thanks, sir."

"Why not?" he frowned.

"Ugh-"

"Look, I know you don't need it, but you deserve it, really. Just think about it." He reached down and pulled out a white envelope. "Here you go," grinned Shelly.

"Thank you," I replied, standing up.

"No questions or anything before you go?"

After about a second of thought, I said no and reached out for a handshake with my free hand. Once this firm exchange came to an end, I left the office, proceeding home.

ΔΔΔ

"A representative of the Technological Enhancement Organization is attempting cellular communication with you. Would you like to accept?" asked my Extension.

"Yeah," I replied, making myself comfortable on the best seat our porch had to offer. Just as millions of others around the country, I'd upgraded to this metal, bracelet-like device, crafted in such a manner as to snugly fit the wrist of whoever its user was.

"Mr. Busara?" said a familiar lady's voice through the speaker.

"Yup."

"Great, well lets get right into it," she said. "We're willing to offer you and your brother upwards of $5 million in the first year of your contract."

"Really?!" I asked, astonished.

"That's right, Mr. Busara. What do you say?"

I remained silent, considering things.

"You still there, Mr. Busara?"

"Oh yeah, sorry. I'm just wondering about the contract terms. Like how long we'll be under it and everything."

"As of now, we've got you down for the 5 year minimum plus a probable extension. But if there's any concern on your part during that period, you can withdraw from the contract early; You'll just have to turn over any inventions we invested in."

"You mean like-"

"We can claim anything you work on with TEO money or resources if you opt out," she continued.

"Well we'll have to get back to you on that," I replied, recognizing this huge red flag.

"Something wrong?" she asked.

"No," I said firmly. "We just need time to think."

"I understand there's a lot to think about, sir, but I need a yes or no from you and your partner."

My issue with their initial offer certainly wasn't the money coming our way, but rather the idea of being trapped under contract due to such a one-sided policy. The entire thing reeked of a big- no - *the biggest* corporation in the world cashing in and stealing our creative freedom.

"Can you make any exceptions on the opt out policy?"

"I'm afraid not, sir, but we could definitely raise the starting salary if it hel-"

"Call ended," said my Extension immediately after my button press. A deal with TEO was clearly out of the question given what I'd come to discover. So what if they were on top of our dad's list of investors and corporations? There were plenty others who'd gladly throw money at us under our terms. I stood up and groaned with frustration, keeping it down enough not to be heard by Jabari, while going inside. The basement door shut harder than expected as I darted through it and down the stairs where our work space awaited. While I truly wasn't in a working mood, I needed something to feel good about, and productivity always did the trick. But just as I took a seat on the stool, the door opened.

"What're you doing?" Bari yelled down to me.

"Just working for a bit," I mistakenly sighed.

"Oh, hold up, I'll be down in a minute!"

For what!? I screamed on the inside. He hadn't stepped foot down there since the funeral but now had a change of heart right at the wrong time. I started to grab our bag of things beneath the table when Bari returned, stumbling down the stairs.

"What's that?" I asked, eyeing the box he had in hand. With a smirk, he slid the rectangular top off and sent dominoes crashing across the table. "Just found them earlier," he said. "Let's get some games in real quick." Despite being the opposite of how I intended to spend my evening, robbing Bari and myself of what now were sparse bonding opportunities wasn't an option. "Alright," I said, "wash 'em."

Bari flipped the metal-dotted chips face down and shuffled them in a circle, pushing the pile towards me once he finished. Amongst the several dominoes I snagged for myself, lied the double six which granted me the first turn. After placing it down, I was immediately followed up by Bari with a six-three of his own. I scanned my hand and groaned as it already wasn't a good one.

"Going fishing?" Bari teased.

I picked through fourteen spare dominoes off to the side in search of either a three or six. The first chip was a no-go, so I tried again with an identical result. Bari snickered beside me until I pulled a six-two from the pile, placing it down.

"Lucky."

"Just go," I said. It was bad enough I had two extra chips to try to get rid off; his badgering was the last thing I wanted to hear.

"Don't blame me cause you picked a sorry hand," he laughed.

"I hope you know you suck, bro."

"That's why I always beat you right?"

"Literally, you just get lucky every time," I point out.

"Chill, you're supposed to lose to your big bro anyway."

"You act like I didn't teach you how to play."

"Pretty sure dad did."

"Pretty sure he was on like trip number 20 of the week when I taught you!" I fired back.

"I mean, it *was* his job; not like he could just stay home 24/7."

"Just go," I fussed.

He finally took his turn, but I was still sizzling until a few phases later, when I managed to catch up, having one remaining chip to his two. It was now his move, and he groaned before fishing for yet another domino from the pile. His look of relief at what he got told me it was a viable chip. I could only pray he'd place it opposite to where I needed mine to win.

"I'm out," I smirked, as he did just that.

Bari doubled back like he wanted to flip the table as I laughed on. Despite now being in better spirits, I restrained myself from offering a rematch and hoped he'd take his loss in peace.

"Got lucky, bro," said Bari, tossing his last two dominoes and walking out.

To kick off this much needed solitude, I sloppily brushed every domino into the box, and retrieved our bag of tools and creations from beneath the table. First out was the Electric Discharge Pistol (EDP) which could generate and fire raw energy to shock and stun targets. Then came my personal favorite of the two, the Electromagnetic Stasis Grenade (ESG), meant to pull objects within its activation radius into a floating bubble of energy above. I reached back in for our pouch and felt around the inside without even taking it out, grasping the two screws needed.

As usual, I very carefully opened the ESG, avoiding another unsafe reaction between the pair of orbs inside containing chemical compounds. They each sat snugly in their own minuscule pod, converging energy up through the center to form the stasis bubbles. But this was only intended to happen upon pressing the activation button, which we'd realized wasn't the case a few days prior when Bari was randomly snatched up and dropped. While it wasn't the most daunting one-man job, I thought better of it and moved on to the EDP, cracking it right open as it didn't require as timid an approach. We'd crafted it so once the trigger was squeezed, a spark would be created for the barrel to quickly absorb and shoot out with immense velocity, taking the form of an electric sphere. Of course, this type of blast wasn't solely produced by the tiny spark on its own; the barrel actually had grooves laced with superconductors, making for formidable shots. After quickly going through my routine checkup, I got down to business.

The trigger frame was a bit too loose, but this was nothing a few screw cranks couldn't fix. Then I locked in on the main issue of calibrating for delay, only to remember my laptop was upstairs. Bari's name nearly left my mouth until I thought better of it and went myself.

"That was like five minutes!" called Bari from the kitchen. But I was already halfway up to my room where the laptop awaited. "You heard?" he persisted.

The hell? I said to myself, searching everywhere as footsteps neared by the second.

"You couldn't hear me calling you?"

I shook my head without turning.

"Well I don't know what's up with your laptop, so could you help?"

I somehow stayed composed all the way back downstairs, but sighed up a storm upon seeing the unresponsive device.

"Why'd you have my laptop anyway? Where's yours?"

"Charging," he said much to my distaste.

"Ok?"

"I'm not gonna use it while it's charging and screw up my battery. Probably why yours is fried now."

"What's fried?" I asked, rubbing the now lit up screen in his face.

"Thanks," he reached.

"I need it; just wait and use yours."

Bari frowned. "Don't be like that, bro."

"I gotta calibrate for delay," I blurt out.

"Oh, that's easy, we could knock that out real quick and then I'll hop back on."

Quietly mourning my now lost alone time overshadowed any interest in what he even wanted with my laptop. "C'mon," I trudged.

Once downstairs he asked, "Which one's even got a delay?"

"The EDP," I said, syncing it to the laptop. It then occurred to me that I could salvage a thought or two to myself by letting Bari take care of it. He was clearly bored out of his mind anyway, so I slid everything to his half of the table and he was off to the races.

He'd always been a bit better than I with these things anyway, but that was to be expected given both our age difference and how pliable he was granting far more time with my father. I'd hover around a bit while my dad worked, but never took it seriously enough for him to gravitate towards me as he did Bari.

"Nothing's up with the storage space right?"

"No," I tapped back in.

"No corrupt file or nothing?"

"Nope, probably just didn't give the calibration changes time to register before I logged off last time."

"Oh yeah, probably," he nodded.

Our dynamic had plenty of time to flourish over the years, as business trip after business trip left the lab open not only for us to conceive and work tirelessly on our creations, but for me to come into my own.

He tossed the EDP at me. "Should be good now."

"Lemme see." I assured our usual concrete target across the room was stable before squeezing the trigger. There was warmth against my hand as the chemicals and mini conductors produced energy which I only semi-charged before blasting. "Yeah, it's good." So good, in fact, I let off a few more shots until the cartridge needed to be refilled for the first time in about two weeks.

Awaiting my go-ahead, Bari hovered over the laptop

and, the instant he got it, I was finally left by my lone-
some.

CHAPTER 2: LIFTOFF

I sat at my bedside anxiously awaiting the arrival of a visitor who, frankly, was unwanted given my presumption with regard to our "brief meetings" purpose. My lamp on the nightstand directly next to me provided more than enough light within the small space around it, yet next to none for the remaining areas. Given the fact that my heart had begun its journey to my stomach, the four walls surrounding me uncharacteristically failed to grasp my attention with their semi-hypnotic design consisting of abstractly decorated planks placed vertically and lined up adjacently, each separated by thin shaded creases on either side. These minuscule spaces served the purpose of pumping air into the room, providing optimal temperatures at the turn of a knob. I glanced down at the 6 year old framed photo on my nightstand of myself and Bari at ages 17 and 19 respectively, standing on either side of our father's Mark 1 Strider which sat on our backyard grass. This variation of his invention was a far cry from the full-fledged androids made available to the world once he perfected his creation, doing their part to improve everyday life. Despite there being numerous proto- types after it, the Mark 1 was the only one that our dad actually held on to following the final products release. Success didn't inspire our dad to upgrade from the home he and our mom raised us in though; and I had no qualms about this since the area had such a low crime rate in addition to only seeming to im- prove year after year. Our father's Striders were in such high demand worldwide due to their capability to be programmed for practically any job. But, even this ridiculous amount of financial security failed to overcome my thirst for independence, so I kept work- ing part-time at Shelly's. We'd also opted out of using our father's vast wealth for anything with relation to inventing, exclusively spending it on bills and food. This was no excuse, however, for the struggle to find our own success and, ultimately, leave a mark as big as our father had on the world. I found it hilariously deflating that even dad's lifeless precursors to his ultra-successful finished product equated to far more than any combined effort Bari and I made at being im- pactful. Recognizing myself getting worked up at the thought of this, I forced my gaze away from the photo. Due to my very probable prediction that my visitor would arrive barring execrable news, I wished to have a good friends consolation nearby. I stood up lazily and walked across the fluffy terrain of my dim-green carpet to the wooden desk within the rooms corner west of my television where I then glanced down at my lifeless cell phone before grabbing the Extension from its place adjacent to it. I placed my hand betwixt it and pushed the largest of three buttons on its side, causing three clicking sounds and the screen to illuminate. I felt a subtle tingle as it tightened and multiple blue streaks of light made their way from the Extension to my head. "Please stand by while I prepare for use," said an authentically snazzy voice. It waited a few moments before proceeding, "Syncing with host. Loading...Loading...Loading...Syncing complete. Preparing cellular communication for use. Preparing telepathic communication for use. All central applications ready for use. Now preparing user-installed applications. Loading...loading...user-installed applications ready for use. All applications ready for use."

I pushed the second largest button on its side.

"Please provide a command."

"Call Ivanna," I replied.

"Would you like to make this call using cellular or telekinetic communication?" asked the Extension.

"Cellular."

"Calling Ivanna."

After about 10 seconds of ringing, I heard Ivanna's voice from the Extensions speaker say, "Hello?"

"Are you and your dad working today?" I asked.

"No, the clinic's closed on Saturday."

"Oh yeah," I told her, playing off my bad memory. "Can you come over in a little while?"

"Yeah," she replied swiftly, neglecting to even request a reason why. "I'll take the train over there."

"Ok, see you in a bit."

"See ya," she said just before ending the call.

I turned to leave my room, and saw the closed door of my parents room straight across the hall as I walked toward the door. I'd only been in their room once since the crash. I stepped from the rug of my room onto the wood floor of the hallway, turned left, and placed a hand on the glossy frame of the entrance to Jabari's room directly next door to peek in. Unsurprisingly, he hid everything excluding his head beneath his covers while asleep. Bari's routine afternoon nap would be cut off by the shriek of his alarm in due time.

The doorbell abruptly rang, prompting me to scramble down the nearby staircase, stomping on the livingrooms hardwood floor and anxiously approach the front door. Upon opening it, I encountered an incredibly cold breeze alongside my expected guest, Abram, who was one of many investors I'd been in contact with from our dad's list.

Abram's beard was unusually fluffy but his spectacles were consistent in resting on the tip of his nose. "Hi, Naaji," he said.

"Hey, what's going on?" I asked, inviting him into my abode.

He entered, let out a heavy sigh, and said, "Can we sit?"

"Of course," I replied as cordially as possible. We sat on couches adjacent to one another.

"Naaji, at this point, I've got no choice but to pull the plug on you and your brother."

"What happened?" I asked, knowing full well what

the answer was.

"Well, to be honest, I haven't seen anywhere near the productivity you promised when I agreed to fund you and your brother. And at this point, it feels like you're playing me for a fool."

"No! It's not like that at all," I promised. "Just please give us another chance.

"Naaji, I've given you more than enough funding, time, and chances but I've seen no improvement or seriousness," said Abram. "I'm sorry about your folks; I *really* am, but I can't keep wasting time and resources without any results.

It was a tough pill to swallow, but I certainly could not blame him.

"I'm sorry, sir," I said.

"So am I, Naaji, but we're done," replied Abram, rising from his seat to leave. I sprang up from the couch and led him to the front door, only to be met by an even more bitter gust of wind than the former as Abram turned to shake my hand and I met him halfway. "I wish you both the best," he said before I shut the door and grabbed my pair of boots from our nearby shoe rack, and sat back down. To get the first coal black boot on, I cuffed my left lower jean leg to squeeze into it and knot its laces followed by doing the same to the other side. It was then that I stood back up and re-trieved my forest green weatherproof jacket from the coat rack near our front door to compliment the grey hoodie I already had on, made my way onto the front deck, and took a seat, where I always did, in the only non-rocking chair on the far side of it with the least amount of creaking planks to await Ivanna's arrival. Our block was always popular with a constant flow of passing cars and that day was no exception as I scanned each one that cruised by, struggling to actually see actual drivers or passengers due to my mediocre eyesight. This lasted for some time until she made it to our house and up onto the deck. I quickly forced a smile to conceal any trace of disappointment upon my face. She had on a puffy brownish-green coat and jeans that very lightly hugged her curves, leading down her feet which were contained by what appeared to be a brand new pair of sneakers.

The deck subtly moaned as Ivanna walked along it to take her seat next to me. "You ok?" she asked, seeing right through my veil.

"Me and Bari just lost an investor," I sighed.

"What? Why!?"

"I kinda oversold how productive we'd be," I replied. She was visibly annoyed.

"I know; I messed up."

Ivanna paused to think of what to say to me next.

"I don't think me and Bari can do it," I said.

"What do you mean?"

"We can't get our own big invention out there like my dad did."

"Of course you can," assured Ivanna. "Its big shoes to fill, obviously, but not impossible. You're just frustrated is all."

As usual, she made great points.

"I mean, you owe it to yourself to at least finish what you started before you try to quit. And Jabari too," she added. "What's he up to anyway? Moping around like you?"

"He doesn't even know yet," I meekly replied.

"Well how's he been since the funeral?"

"Not too good. He's having a hard time getting past it."

Ivanna swiftly shifted her expression to a more empathetic one. "He sounds just like me when my mom passed. Took me way longer than my dad to move on."

"Yeah," I said just before hearing a notification within my mind from my Extension.

"A representative of the Technological Enhancement Organization would like to Telepathically communicate with you."

Given how overly persistent the organization had been up until then, I decided to put both them and myself out of our misery. "Hold on, I got a call," I told Ivanna before saying in my mind, "Answer call," limiting my hearing to the bounds of my head. "Hello?"

A man who's throat I could swear was laced with gravel replied, "Hello, Mr. Busara. How are you?"

"Great!" I lied. "You?"

"I'm fine. Just wondering why you haven't been answering any of our calls since the last one failed.

I froze, thinking of how to respond.

"Hello?" called the man.

"Yeah!" I uh- you guys called?"

"Yes. Plenty of times actually," said the man stiffly.

"Sorry about that," I laughed, "we've just had a lot on our plates lately."

"The organization understands that, but we need for you and your brother to come to our central headquarters in New York to seal our partnership."

"We would love to do that, but we're gonna have to decline for now."

"May I ask why that is?"

"We have lots of options to weigh first," I lied once again.

"I can assure you, Mr. Busara, our contract is the best one you'll find," said the man.

"Thank you, but no thank you." This exchange was the epitome of interactions between TEO and I.

"Listen, sir!" he snarled. "You can either come to New York like we asked, or we can send someone to negotiate in person."

I was jarred by this statement for a moment until finally replying, "Was that a threat?"

"What do you think, Mr. Busara?"

I saw Ivanna suddenly dart from her seat beside me and into the house as if she heard the chilling turn the call had taken.

"End call," I told my Extension verbally before rushing after Ivanna to see what had caused her reaction, only to find her tending to Bari as he layed motionless on the livingroom floor. "What's going on?!"

"I think he just fainted," Ivanna nonchalantly replied, tugging the collar of Bari's sweat-stained t-shirt away from his neck.

"Well what do we do?!" I squealed.

"You gotta calm down!" she snapped. "Help me get his legs up."

I knelt down and followed her lead, lifting my brothers left leg as she elevated the other until his toes hovered above his chest. We held the dead weight of his lower half which was contained by a silky pair of grey sweatpants for what felt like an eternity until, finally, Bari gasped while unsealing the lids covering his suntanned pupils.

"You alright?!" I asked whilst slowly sitting him up.

He appeared more relieved to see me than he was to have regained consciousness. "Where were you? I thought you were gone," he gasped.

"Relax," Ivanna ordered whilst checking his heartbeat.

"When do I ever leave without letting you know?" I asked rhetorically.

Bari sat silent, offering a look of shame for himself rather than a verbal response.

"Help him up," Ivanna cut in before she and I each grabbed one of Bari's hands to lift and help him onto the couch. "Don't get up for a few minutes."

"Yeah she's right, Bari. Sit down and we'll get you something for your head," I added, signaling Ivanna to follow me into the kitchen.

"My head's fine," he whined.

"No it's not!" I replied, agitated. "Just listen to us."

"My bad, jeez."

Ivanna and I proceeded to enter the kitchen where I was immediately greeted by our turquoise personal Strider which raised its head saying, "Hello, Mr. Busara. May I be of any assistance?"

"Not now," I replied far more sternly than necessary.

"Very well, sir." It returned to rest mode.

Ivanna wasted no time addressing what she'd just witnessed. "You didn't tell me he was this bad," she whispered.

"Look, I'm just as surprised as you, but that's not what I brought you in here for."

"What could be more important?" she challenged.

"Somebody from TEO just threatened me on a call," I replied.

"What did they say?"

"Me and Bari have to either meet with them, or he's gonna send somebody here to do something to us."

Ivanna looked visibly shaken.

"But don't tell Bari. He's dealing with enough already."

"Don't tell me what?" asked Bari, both startling and sending me into a moment of thought about my response.

"We lost our investor."

"Why!?" he cried.

"He said we weren't productive enough."

Bari's face was momentarily enveloped by disappointment until he appeared to reach a realization. "We still got the other investor though, right?"

"Which other one?" I asked, knowing full-well who he referred to.

"TEO."

"Oh yeah; it doesn't don't look too good for that either."

"What are we supposed to do now, then?" Bari groaned.

"We'll figure something out, but for now you need to just go relax upstairs."

Before exiting the kitchen, Bari gave me a subtle nod of agreement before leaving the kitchen, closely followed by the sound of him scurrying upstairs. This granted me much needed relief from the veil of pretending not to be just as stressed out as him.

"You should call the police," said Ivanna.

"Call local police station," I told my Extension.

"Calling local police station."

It only took one ring for me to get an answer. "Jersey City Police Station; how can I help you today?"

"I got a threatening call from TEO and-"

Nothing but static was heard through my Extensions speaker.

"Hello? Hello?!"

"Call disconnected," said my Extension. "Would you like to-"

"Yes, call back."

"Calling back."

Two rings came and went, before a voicemail played: "I'm sorry, sir or ma'am, but the Jersey City Police Station hotline is experiencing technical difficulties. The service will be back online as soon as possible. Please call back at another time."

I resorted to calling 9-1-1, only to receive no answer at all. "We gotta get outta here."

"And go where?" asked Ivanna.

"Not sure yet, but anywhere that's not here. At least until we know it's safe to come back."

"They have your address?"

"Yup; we're screwed."

"Why don't you just stay with us in Bayonne? In the guest room."

This was music to my ears. "Would your dad be cool with it."

"I'll call to check, but I'm pretty sure he'll let you." She then pressed the voice command button on her Extension. "Call dad."

"Because this contact is on a cell phone, cellular communication is the only option for this call. Would you like to continue anyway?" asked the Extension.

"Yes."

"Very well. Calling dad."

In all my years of being close friends with Ivanna, the only thing I managed to pick up on with regard to her father was their shared spirituality.

"What's up, sweetie?" asked a soft-spoken voice through the speaker.

Ivanna wasted no time trying to butter him up. "Hey, dad, can Naaji and Jabari stay with us for awhile?"

Without even seeking a reason for such a request, he replied, "Yeah, of course. Just tell them the guest rooms only got one bed."

"Ok," replied Ivanna, looking over at me to ensure I got the memo. "Thanks dad."

"No problem. See you soon."

"See ya," she replied. "End call."

"Call ended."

Now that there was somewhere for us to hide out, I wished to leave immediately.

"Lets go tell Bari the news," I said, exiting the kitchen

to the living-room.

"Alright."

My parents weren't the type to blow even a modest portion of their wealth on unnecessary things, so our home was by no means what most probably expected. This preference was understandable considering we almost never entertained guest outside of family; and even those visits became increasingly scarce over time for reasons unbeknownst to me. I rested my hand on the banister and hurried up the staircase at my usual pace of two steps at a time with Ivanna following close behind. Our simultaneous yet differing stomps produced a sound that was rough on the ears. Once we reached the top, I made my way to and stepped in Bari's doorway, where he was resting feebly in bed.

"Hey, Bari."

"What's up?"

"You feel alri-"

"Yeah," he replied, sitting up.

"Good, cause we're about to go to Ivanna's house."

"How come?"

"We need some time away to figure things out."

Bari took a moment to think. "We're leaving right now you mean?"

"Once we pack up."

He switched his gaze to Ivanna. "You asked your dad already?"

"Yeah, he's fine with you staying."

He took this into consideration before replying, "I'll be ready in a bit."

The minimal effort taken to get Bari on board was a pleasant surprise. "Me too. Just go downstairs when you're done," I said, exiting the room while he got out of bed.

"I'll wait downstairs," Ivanna told me.

"Cool, we'll be down soon." I stepped into my room and went straight for my closet. Thankfully, I gave each of my outfits its own hanger, allowing me to grab the entire rotation of clothes in one shot and lay it across the bed. Everything fit nicely into one of two duffel bags which were close at hand. Next up on my list of things to pack were underclothes. I practically emptied the triple-stacked bins against my rooms east wall, pulling two weeks worth of tank-tops, boxers, and socks from it and transferring everything to the second duffel bag. My keys and wallet were nearby, so I grabbed them as well. Then, I hurried to grab both my toothbrush and favorite mouthwash which was free of the mouth-scorching contents found in most contemporaries. "What else?" I whispered to myself, tossing both items into the underclothes bag. Our ESGs and EDPs swiftly came to mind, and refusing to risk having them stolen while we were away, I made my way to the staircase and ran down to retrieve them.

"Done already?" asked Ivanna, glancing inquisitively from the living-room couch, in search of any bags in my possession.

"Nah, I'm just getting our prototypes."

"Oh. Well don't forget to pack a blowup bed," she said, simultaneously returning to whatever her Extension had her occupied with.

I opened the door to the basement. "I won't." Due to much of our father's time being spent down there, he always ensured the space remained well-kept, thus my nose was kissed but sweet lavender rather than typical basement mustiness upon entry. Even the stairs refrained from sobbing as loudly as our front porch ones would when I stumbled down them. Our ESGs, EDPs, and the extensive set of tools used to develop them sat on a wooden table in the rooms center next to our dad's Mark 1 Strider and surrounded by countless scraps from our own many failed attempts at successful creations. I pulled my backpack from underneath the table and surgically separated throughout its many compartments, everything we needed, one at a time to ensure each item was unscathed. Being that this was its debut, a satisfyingly crisp sound unveiled itself from the bag, upon being zipped shut. I tested its ability to contain the many items by lifting it up and down a few times by the straps until finding this to be a satisfactory carrying device, at which point, I swung it onto my back. It was then that I scrambled out of the basement, two steps at a time, shut its door behind myself, and saw Ivanna still in the same position as before with the addition of Bari, making his way toward the front door with only a single duffel bag in hand.

"What're you doing?" I asked.

"Putting my stuff in the car." Bari now wore a bulky ruby-red jacket, unzipped to reveal the forest-green hoodie on the interior, an alternate pair of sweatpants to before, sporting their brand name down the left leg, as well as a pair of beige boots.

"That's all your taking?"

"Yeah what else do i need?" he frowned.

"We're staying in Bayonne for more than a day or two, so you need more than whatever's in that bag."

"Naaji's right," Ivanna intervened. "My dad's gonna let you stay as long as you need to."

"Why are we staying so long anyway?" he asked, causing my heart to sink.

"You need time to get back on track," replied Ivanna.

"I guess," he replied before retreating upstairs.

"Thanks," I quietly said to Ivanna followed by going upstairs behind him. I retrieved the already packed bags from my room and proceeded to our hallway closet, containing numerous things including the blowup bed which was already stuffed into the carrying bag that'd accompanied it when purchased alongside the air pump. I held the bed in my left hand and the other two bags in my dominant one. Bari was scrambling to pack when I glanced into his room while passing, to reach the stairway, and the moment I reached the bottom, Ivanna motioned me toward her.

"What's up?"

"We should take the bullet train instead of your car."

"What for?" I asked.

"If they're really after you, its better to leave the car in the driveway so it's not so obvious you guys are leaving town," she said.

"You sure?"

"Yeah. And I mean, if anything, we've got my dads van."

Bari came crashing downstairs with just as many bags as I. "Time to go?"

"Yup," replied Ivanna. "We're taking the train though."

"Why not the car?"

"There's not really anywhere to park around my house."

"Whatever I guess," he submitted on his way to the door.

Ivanna proceeded after him and I behind her. Bari doubled back.

"Forgot something?" asked Ivanna.

"Nah; lets go."

I shut the door behind the three of us and we began our march to the train station just down my block. We were positioned side-by-side, taking up the entirety of space offered by our streets narrow sidewalk. There were plenty of things (good and bad) for Bari and I to get ourselves into where we grew up, but, fortunately for us, our minds were far too stayed on following our dads passion for the latter to stand any chance. The spotlight and I were never acquaintances,so it was a godsend that we'd already passed the phase of tender-aged kids by the time his masterpiece was complete which of course generated boat-loads of media attention.

I pushed the command button on my Extension, saying, "When's the next train to Bayonne coming?"

"According to the schedule of the nearest bullet-train

station to you, the estimated time of arrival for that train is three minutes."

"Thanks."

"My pleasure sir," replied my Extension.

This exchange was more than enough to prompt us to put a bit extra pep in our step. We were forced to momentarily walk single-file past a few approaching pedestrians. This change of position was perfectly timed since I had the pleasure of being at least partially shielded behind both Bari and Ivanna whilst a freezing blast of wind whistled by.

Bari mumbled something under his breath as we neared the station.

"Huh?" I asked.

"I said of course it's crowded."

"It *is* the weekend," replied Ivanna.

I saw some familiar faces from around my neighborhood awaiting trains from both directions within the area up a nearby ramp. To join the small crowd, we cautiously stepped over a set of tracks and up the ramp.

"Train to Bayonne incoming! Please stand clear of all areas near the tracks," the intercoms shrieked simultaneously. The train could be seen and heard arriving on the side of the station adjacent to where we stood as its zoom sizzled out to a stop. We rushed to purchase our tickets from three different machines as people both standing and sitting alike flocked for seats, showing little to no regard for those attempting to exit.

I was no more courteous, slipping into their ranks

with the others in tow. Assuming the car that seemed to swallow the least amount of people would be ripe with empty seats for us to sit together was a mistake. As the dust settled, unoccupied seats became even more scarce, forcing our trio to split. Ivanna found refuge a few rows from the cars rear while I managed to secure a spot toward the front. The two duffel bags were on the floor between my legs while I hugged the backpack on my lap. The man beside me took up more space on the seats than he was intended to, but I was just content to have a seat at all. Bari, and a handful of others, weren't so fortunate and would have to spend the short ride standing.

Regardless of our governments typical overthinking and common sense, they somehow failed to make accommodations for those forced to stand up. On the flip side everyone sitting needed to deposit their ticket into a slot below their seat in order for their seatbelts to be activated. This system didn't do much to alleviate the issue of people taking free rides though.

"This train will depart in twenty seconds," the intercom notified us. "Please insert your tickets into the ticket slot below your seats to unlock the seatbelts for use. Once, unlocked, please buckle and tighten them snugly."

We all followed its instructions, resulting in a sudden symphony of metal clicks. I'd also come to the realization that Bari had wasted his money on a ticket he couldn't even use. It went without saying he wouldn't be getting a refund for it either.

"Now departing."

The train took little to no time to reach top speed, at which point, I felt my stomach briefly squirm with discomfort. Bullet trains had been around for a year and change, but this was only my third or fourth go-around on one since we had a car for venturing around. The raw speed which made them such a hit amongst people without the convenience of a car was on full display.

"You've now entered Bayonne, New Jersey," said the intercom as we slowed to a stop, shifting everyone who stood forward. All doors reopened and a decent chunk of passengers stood to depart as I, foreseeing a collision due to my bags, remained seated until they passed by with Ivanna being the exception.

She pointed to my bags. "Want me to get one?"

"No thanks."

I stood with my things, and prompted her to proceed ahead of me. Those of us exiting the train outweighed the people entering from this stop.

"All applications synced with your current location," my Extension telepathically notified me as Bari, who was waiting nearby, joined Ivanna and I. The three of us were barely out of the station when I began to regret turning down Ivanna's offer to give me a hand with the bags which felt heavier by the moment.

"How far's your house?" asked Bari as if having noticed the strain I was under.

"Not too far. Why? You alright?"

"Yeah; just curious," he replied as Ivanna then led us on our journeys final stretch.

CHAPTER 3: MR. ABIAH

B eing so acclimated to both the creak-prone nature and practical instability of my own porch, I made sure to tread gently along Ivanna's which ended up lacking such issues anyway. As she approached the door with her key, I was overcome with joy at the thought of finally being relieved of my burdensome luggage. We followed Ivanna into our temporary home only to immediately be bombarded by her dad. "Hey guys," he said. Mr. Abiah shared Bari's low cut style of hair and beard, but his was a gray tundra. He had a chestnut skin tone, and wide-bridged nose with minimal apex protrusion. The velvety black robe flowing down to his ankles was clearly for some sort of religious ceremony.

I reached for a hand shake, saying, "Hey, Mr. Abiah," but instead received a warm embrace which Bari soon found himself treated to as well. We were squished within his grasp.

Once we were given space to breath, he jovially said, "Just call me Isaiah," and followed it up by asking what brought us there.

"We just need some time away since we lost our investor," I replied. "We'll find somewhere else if it's any trouble though."

He placed a hand on my shoulder. "No trouble. Stay as long as you need to. There *are* a few house rules, but we'll talk about those later."

"Cool," said Bari.

"Oh, you guys can just sit your bags by the couch for now." We complied before he continued, "You're actually right on time for church; you should come for a little while." This proposition seemed fair given the huge favor being done for us, however, as Bari looked to me, awaiting a response, I scrambled for an excuse to weasel out of taking part in this unfamiliar activity, but clearly not fast enough.

"Naaji?"

"Huh?"

"You're fine with going, right?" he pressed.

"Yeah, we'll go for a bit," I submitted.

"Great! Let's head over there before we're late," he said, leading us outside where his glossy seven-seater awaited.

CHAPTER 4: PROPHETS

U pon entering the church we were met by a great deal of people on all sides before Isaiah made us aware of his position as Bishop, pointing down the aisle to four men sitting at a long table on stage, each having a microphone and what appeared to be bibles in front of them. I hardly got to admire the church's scale and beautiful stained-glass windows before he proceeded to reveal their names starting from the left: Deacon Daniel, Deacon Joel, Deacon Ezekial, and Deacon Obadiah. They all sport fully developed beards, ranging from ear to ear, and are wearing black robes identical to Isaiah in addition to dark skin pigmentations almost identical to one another. Deacon Daniel had a patch of hair missing that left a bald area ranging from where his hairline likely used to be to just past the horizon separating the top and back of his head. His nose had a condensed bridge and wide apex. Deacon Joel's hairdo consisted of countless dreadlocks tied neatly to the rear of his head. His nose was fleshy at both the bridge and apex. Deacon Ezekial was sporting a humongous afro that touched his ears, and a nose which was thin all throughout with a break toward the top of the right nostril. Deacon Obadiah had all the hair of his head shaded to a nearly bald state except for the top which seemed to be intentionally nappy, in addition to a minuscule but flat nose.

"You can have a seat anywhere you like," Isaiah told us with a smile before making his way down the aisle to the stage. I briefly scanned the sea of people packed into the rows of seats on either side of the aisle before leading Bari and Ivanna to the few open seats just a few rows from the very back. After sitting down, I looked toward the stage and saw that Isaiah had now taken his seat at the table in between the other men just before hearing him speak loudly through the towering speakers both in front and back of the building, saying, "We have special guests in our congregation this beautiful afternoon."

This sent a stir through the crowd.

"Please welcome our guests Naaji and Jabari to the church on this blessed Sabbath day."

Everyone began to cheer and clap but thankfully didn't come to realize we were the ones whom they applauded while I gently nudged Ivanna to ask for a reminder of what the Sabbath even is.

"Its the time from sunset Friday to sunset Saturday!" she replied as I struggled to hear her over the crowds roar. "No work's allowed. You can only do stuff like read the bible, group bible study, spend time with family and friends, relax, eat, sleep, and nature walks!"

"Thank you everyone. Now, lets jump right into it," he said, opening his bible and skimming through its pages. He waited until the crowd grew silent. "Deuteronomy 28:47-51 states, 'Because thou does not serve The Most High thy god with joyfulness, and with gladness of heart, for the abundance of all things; Therefore shalt thou serve thine enemies which the Lord shall send against thee, in hunger, and in thirst, and in nakedness, and in want of all things. And he shall put a yoke of iron upon thy neck, until he have destroyed thee. The Lord shall bring a nation against thee from far, from the end of the earth, as swift as the eagle flieth. A nation whose tongue thou shalt not understand. A nation of fierce countenance, which shall not regard the person of the old, nor shew favour to the young. And he shall eat the fruit of thy cattle, and the fruit of thy land, until thou be destroyed. They also shall not leave thee either corn, or wine, or oil, or the increase of thy kine, or flocks of thy sheep, until they have destroyed thee.'"

"What's he talking about?" I whispered to Ivanna.

"The bad things Jews went through. And he's about to get into the positive stuff."

"Peter 3:1-2. 'My son, forget not my law, but let thine heart keep my commandments. For length of days, and long life, and peace, shall they add to thee.' Keep in mind that these verses are from the New Testament which a bunch of people, for whatever reason, consider to be anti-commandment even with plenty of verses that say otherwise. Revelation 14:12-13. 'Here is the patience of the saints. Here are they that keep the commandments of The Most High, and the faith of Christ. And I heard a voice from Heaven saying unto me, write, blessed are the dead which die in the Lord from henceforth. Yea, saith the Spirit, that they may rest from their labors, and their works do follow them.' Once again, obeying the commandments is shown to be a necessary component in the journey to the kingdom. And I know we go over this kind of stuff a lot but are there any questions about the topics we just covered?"

Not a soul in the congregation indicated a need for further expounding.

"How about our special guests?" he asked, staring me down from the stage.

I shook my head. "Uh.... no!"

This simple reply sent the crowd into a frenzy which Isaiah waited for the end of before glancing down at his bible, saying, "Lets move on to something new now."

I slapped Bari's wrist and rose from my seat. "C'mon," I told him.

"Where you going?" asked Ivanna.

"We're just gonna go take a walk," I replied, much to her distaste.

"You could just say you're ready to leave. I'll take you back to my house to unpack," she said. "My dad cooked for the Sabbath if you're hungry too; I'll just come back to pick him up when he's done."

"Yeah, let's go," I said. Ivanna stood and we followed her out of the church as stealthily as possible.

CHAPTER 5: HOME AWAY FROM HOME

Ivanna welcomed us in. "So, this is you guy's room," she said. "I'll be in the kitchen."

Space within the room was scarce thanks to the neatly presented twin bed touching the wall with its side and television setup across from one another, leaving only the area between them and around the doorway for us to walk. "You can take the bed, and I got the blowup," I told Bari once Ivanna went downstairs. I figured squeezing it somewhere wasn't too tall a task.

He pulled back a portion of the bedspread, revealing the beds drawers, and sat down. "We can put some of our stuff in the drawers if the closets not enough room," said Bari, pointing to the right of the door. "And then you can put the blow up bed in between my bed and the TV stand."

"Yeah, but can we do all that later? I feel like working on the ESGs and EDPs right now," I replied, retrieving both the prototypes and parts needed for them from my bag.

"Uh- yeah that's cool I guess." Bari knelt down across from me on the floor and we got to work, shuffling through scraps and tools for what we needed and exchanging them amongst ourselves when necessary.

"What are you doing?!" Ivanna startled me.

"Working on some stuff," replied Bari. "What's wrong?"

"You can't do that until the Sabbath's over."

"How come?" I asked, bewildered.

"No works allowed. We just talked about this at church."

I recalled exactly what she referred to yet asked, "We did?" in an attempt to cover for my absent mindedness.

"Yeah; we did," she insisted, "so put all that away until later."

I, followed by Bari, scrambled to do as she said. "Sorry."

"It's alright, just try not to let it happen anymore. Especially around my dad."

"Gotcha," Bari confidently replied.

"He'll tolerate most other stuff, but you'll need to follow the rules of the Sabbath."

I'd never known Ivanna to be a blind follower, so anything she believed upon to this degree, in my mind, had to have some legitimacy. "No problem."

"Thanks," replied Ivanna in the softest tone I'd heard in the interaction before she once again left the room. Bari stood up from the floor, and stepped over me. "I'm gonna go get something to eat."

Following close in tow, I replied, "I'm gonna get some air."

We went downstairs and split up in the livingroom. "Call the Jersey City Police Station," I whispered to my Extension after pushing its command button.

"Would you like to make this call using cellular or telekinetic communication?"

"Telekinetic," I said, nearly knocking over one of two lamp posts positioned on either end of the single couch facing Ivanna's livingroom TV on my way out.

"Calling Jersey City Police Station."

The walls of the room were decked out with what appeared to be biblical quotes which I didn't bother trying to interpret. Out on their condensed porch was only one seating option: a two-seater bench where I then sat.

"Jersey City Police Station; how can I help you today!?" asked a high-pitched male voice in my head.

"Hi, I'm calling about a threat I received earlier today."

"Who threatened you, and how, sir?"

"I got a call from a representative from TEO and he threatened to send someone to my house if I don't take their contract."

"Ok, sir, hold on for a second while I listen to that call through your call log."

"Alright."

"You've been put on hold," my Extension told me. But this didn't last long.

"Sir?" called the man.

"I'm here."

"You said the call was from today right?"

"Yeah."

"There's no call from them in your log."

"There has to be!" I cried. "They just called me today!"

"I need you to calm down sir. The call you're talking about isn't here. Do you know the representatives name you spoke to?"

I pondered momentarily as if I had any clue. "No."

"Well, without any evidence, to back your claim, there's not much for us to do, sir."

"So what does that mean for me then?"

He too froze briefly, then said, "I'm sorry, sir."

Requesting some kind of protection came to mind, but was swiftly thwarted by the fact that it would be accompanied by Bari finding out what was going on. Just prior to manually ending the call and going back inside, I thanked the operator for his attempt at helping and he told me to call back if anything else happened. This deflating turn of events sent me retreating back to our room in search of a distraction. Anything to sway my thoughts. But nothing did the trick, so I tossed Bari's bedspread out of the way, kicked off my shoes and, with hopes of recuperating, forced myself to sleep.

I heard someone call me, cutting my nap short. "Huh?" I grouchily replied, sitting up as sweat engulfed my skin and clothing.

Ivanna was at our door. "Everything alright?" she asked, staring down my numerous stains.

"Yeah, what's up?"

"My dad's going shopping before the store closes. You can come if you want anything for the house."

"Yeah, I'm coming," I said.

"We're ready whenever," she smiled before moving her head to close the door.

"Aye, what's Bari doing?" I called.

"He's in the kitchen! Doesn't feel like going," replied Ivanna from outside the room.

Here we go, I thought. Bari's paranoid nonsense was still in full swing and, without him even knowing it, could bring unwanted attention from Isaiah. I jumped out of bed and quickly threw on my outer layers before meeting everyone in the kitchen.

"You coming, bro?" I asked Bari who was staring into his Extension. He stood near the stove with Isaiah who looked on, likely trying to learn the intricacies of some game Bari had recently downloaded. Almost all of the space on his device was occupied by knowledge-strengthening applications.

"Nah, I'm kinda tired," he replied.

"What do you want from the store?" I huffed.

"I don't know. Whatever I guess."

He was too fixated on his Extension to even look away when he answered; But before I could lose my cool, it was time to go.

Isaiah patted Bari on the back. "Make yourself at home," he smiled. "We'll be back in a bit."

"Yup," said Bari, still typing away as we left him in the kitchen.

Ivanna made a move for the back door, but I beat her to it, evading further conversation with Isaiah up front.

"You could've sat up here, Naaj'. Don't you need more leg room?"

"I'm good," I say, with a smile in case he checks his rear view. Thankfully, my plan worked to perfection as he and Ivanna were so deep in church-related conversation that I might as well have been cloaked the entire ride.

"Why do they do that?" Isaiah sighed.

"I got it, dad," said Ivanna, darting out of the front passenger seat before I thought to move.

She removed the cart someone left in our intended parking space, allowing Isaiah to enter fully. Once he straightened up, I slid the back right door open and quickly tried to take the push cart from Ivanna.

"I got it," she insisted.

"You sure?" I asked, already knowing what reply I'd receive.

"Mhm."

I looked back for Isaiah as we crossed over to the storefronts welcoming light and Ivanna stopped in her tracks to do the same.

"I'll catch up!" I heard him call. "Go ahead." The lack of natural light outside further exasperated my poor eyesight to the point of seeing him as nothing more than a blurry figure.

"What're you getting?" I asked once the double doors split open.

"Not much probably. We're mostly here for *you*."

As indicated by the decent amount of cars outside, this unfamiliar store still buzzed with shoppers despite its imminent closing time. "Where's the breakfast food?"

A hand suddenly appeared over my shoulder, pointing northeast. "That way," replied Isaiah from behind me.

A monotone voice blasted through the intercoms saying, "Attention all shoppers, the store will be closing in fifteen minutes, so please bring any items you have to the nearest register as soon as possible. Thank you."

Unlike most of the other patrons, we immediately speed walked until reaching the froze food aisle.

"Here you go, Naaj'," said Isaiah.

I opened one freezer door and on the other side were shelves of waffles, all different flavors. However, this didn't make my selection a challenging one by any means. I tossed the family pack into the cart and moved on.

"Plain? That's it?" asked Ivanna.

"All the other ones are kinda trash, so yeah."

I picked out varying packs of sausages from another section, fitting both Bari and my own preferences.

"Reminder, all shoppers: we'll be closing soon, so if you haven't already, please go to the nearest open register!"

"Alright, I'm good," I announced, putting the sausages alongside our waffles.

Isaiah reached for the cart. "I'll push," he said, only to receive an identical result to me.

"You sure you don't want anything besides breakfast food?" he asked me.

"Yeah, it's our favorite."

Ivanna playfully rolled her eyes.

"Fair enough," Isaiah grinned.

Up at the register, a man whose face matched the voice previously blasted for all to hear was methodically ringing up a lady's items. I put our things on the conveyor belt and, while awaiting my turn, searched items bunched together on either side of the narrow lane, but found nothing worthwhile.

"See something you like?" Isaiah poked.

"Not really."

"Sir?" the cashier suddenly called.

"Oh, sorry," I replied, stepping up.

He scanned and began bagging my things. "Your total's thirteen dollars and fifty-seven cents."

I pulled a crisp, pre-prepared twenty dollar bill from my pocket and gave it to the cashier who popped open his register and, with a paper shuffle here, and a coin rattle there, gave me my change along with the two bags. "Thanks for shopping with us; have a great night," he waved.

The ride back to their house was a headache- filled blur, the end of which I could not wait for. It had actually reached point where the moment we entered the house, I stored our things, hoping for solitude immediately after.

"Naaji," said Isaiah, stopping me right at our room door.

"Huh?"

"Could you get Bari out here for dinner for me?"

I somehow managed to mask a groan of frustration

with a throat-clearing grunt. "Uh huh," I replied. But, out of nowhere, Bari swung the door open.

"What's up," he said.

"Dinner time," I mumbled.

He looked far more relieved than I; probably due to lack of much to eat all day. "Oh cool."

Isaiah and Ivanna had already stepped through the kitchen door and we followed, only to find it empty.

Bari pointed over at another door frame I hadn't given more than a glance before then. "In there," he said, stepping by to lead the way into a room that was easily the houses warmest. Ivanna murmured at the tables head with her dad until, finally, Isaiah welcomed us to sit wherever we liked before they both walked out. Of the five available chairs, we chose to occupy those left of the head.

"I'm starving," moaned Bari.

Without meaning to, I ignored him and looked around the space which pulled out just as many stops as their living-room with regard to religious items. The cloth dressing their sturdy dinner table was even decked with biblical quotes written in elegant font. Above were crystals bunched together to form a chandelier lighting up the room.

"C'mon y'all!" said Ivanna from the kitchen. Bari halfway tripped, rushing to answer her call, and barely beat me to the doorway as my stomach had been begging for fuel.

Isaiah handed each of us a paper plate saying, "Help yourselves, guys. We got rice, chicken, string beans and mac'n'cheese." Three plastic containers and an aluminum pan sat alongside a few large metal spoons on their countertop. I was busy salivating at the thought of my impending meal while Bari dumped healthy portions from each tupperware onto his plate. Common courtesy kept me from taking anything more than moderate helpings when my turn arrived.

"You can take more you know," said Isaiah. "We got plenty."

Before I knew it, twice as much of everything was on my plate and Bari had his in the microwave. Pop after pop sounded off for some time until he finally snatched it out and

Ivanna directed him to a napkin holder.

"Thanks," said Bari, dashing back to the table while I heated my neatly assembled plate of food for about the same amount of time as him.

"Hey, Jabari!" cried Isaiah.

"Huh?!"

"You didn't start eating yet, right?"

"Uh...nah."

"Good man. Be there in a minute."

I joined Bari in the dining room and just barely held him off from starting before our hosts re-entered, plates in hand.

"Oh, I forgot," Mr. Abiah began, "if you're thirsty there's water bottles in the fridge."

But that was the least of my concerns. Clearing my plate and considering additional options back in our room was top priority. A beverage would only bloat me to an early submission.

"Naaji," said Isaiah, snapping me out of my trance.

"Huh?"

Ivanna, Bari and Isaiah all had eyes locked on me.

"I was just asking if you wanted to do the honors."

My face was doused in obvious confusion which, thankfully, was alleviated by Ivanna.

"I don't think they know any prayers, dad."

"Oh yeah, no," I replied, playing off my previous bewilderment. "Sorry."

"It's all good, Naaj'. Just checking," he said. "Go ahead, sweetie."

Ivanna cleared her throat and bowed her head before starting. "Heavenly father, thank you for everything you've done and everything you do for us. We ask that you bless us with your everlasting light and allow us to do what's right in your sight now and forever."

There was an awkward pause before Isaiah spoke up.

"Lets eat," he grinned, unaware of the onslaught he invited. Once Bari got going, he took chomp after chomp from his plate and didn't even look our way. I saved my breath, knowing it would be wasted trying to slow him down. Plus, it would better serve my cause not to promote any potentially incriminating dinner table conversation.

"So, Naaji-"

Just my luck.

"Huh?" my voice cracked.

"What do you two do, again? I never really knew."

"We build stuff," replied Bari through his mouthful.

"Oh and you get paid by a company for that?"

"Well actually we wanna stay out of contracts for

now, so no," I told him.

"So how do you make your living?"

"I mean, it's kinda just our thing; we haven't made money off it yet," I explained while finally picking into my plate. "Except investments if that counts."

"But something went wrong," Isaiah said.

"Huh?" I asked, despite clearly hearing him.

"Something got messed up with your funding, right?"

"Oh yeah."

"And that's why you wanna stay here a while?" he squinted.

I squirmed in my seat like a fish out of water. "Um...we needed a change of scenery," I squeaked.

"Thanks for dinner!" Bari startled me. He'd completely leveled the food on his plate in record time.

"No seconds?" asked Isaiah.

Bari shook his head and walked out with his plate.

"Just throw it in the sink, I'll wash it."

I desperately wished I could get up and leave too, but Isaiah was all over me and less than a dent was in my plate.

"So, Naaj'," he started back up, "what were you saying?"

"I-"

My mind and body were at odds as I knew something needed to be said, but simply couldn't spit it out with Isaiah staring a hole straight through me.

"You alright, Naaji?"

I shot a look toward Ivanna that begged for help, but to no avail.

"Could I talk to Naaji in private, sweety?"

"Ok," Ivanna replied, taking her plate and leaving the two of us.

"So, what's really going on?"

"What do you m-"

"I want the truth. What're you *really* here for?" he asked. "If you wanna stay, I have to know."

Isaiah had me cornered without any cover story to bail myself out. I tried to quickly come up with something, but another lie would only serve to dig an even deeper hole for myself.

"TEO threatened us," I whimpered.

"That big company, you mean?"

"Yeah."

"How? What'd they say?" asked Isaiah.

"Basically, if we don't agree to take their contract offer, somebody's getting sent to our house."

Isaiah's eyes widened. "And I assume you called the cops, right?"

"Yeah, but they couldn't even find the recording of the call," my voice cracked. I don't know what to do."

"Well isn't there some protection program you can go to for stuff like this?"

"Bari's already stressed out enough; I'm not putting him through that." My throat tightened. "I get it if you want us to leave."

"Aye," Isaiah waved, "calm down. I'm not kicking you guys out; we just gotta take it a step at a time."

I glanced up, sending tears speeding downward. "Don't tell him about this," I pleaded.

After he stared off to the side of me for a moment, Isaiah refocused and reluctantly said, "Alright," coming around the table to lift me up. "C'mon."

"Where?" I quickly brushed my face dry in case we ran into Bari or Ivanna.

"I wanna show you something real quick."

The coast being clear as we cut through the kitchen and living room thankfully granted extra time to blink and swipe any remaining tears from my eyes. However, I couldn't guess what change of scenery Isaiah had in mind until reaching the second floor hallway where he pulled down a panel above our heads, revealing stairs.

"After you," he pointed. I tested each steps stability before fully committing, and was warned to be careful as a pitch black space lied atop them where Isaiah then joined me closing the entrance behind him. My eyes didn't have the chance to truly adjust which prevented the light he clicked on from stunning me. It *did* however, reveal the space we now stood in: an almost completely empty attic with nothing more than two purple mats placed on either side of the rooms center.

"What's this?" I asked.

"Ever meditate before?"

"Nope."

"Well I want you to try it now, cause it's relaxing, it lets you reflect on stuff, it helps you focus, it - lots of stuff. And it always helps me when I do it."

While I wasn't sure of anything he'd just said, I needed to stay in his good graces now more than ever. "Which one do I sit on?"

"Doesn't matter."

My butt subtly sank into the mat when I sat down.

"Indian style," Isaiah added. Once I was properly situated, he plopped across from me. "Ready?"

"I guess."

"Close your eyes and breathe."

I did as he said.

"No, not like that. Just breathe normally. Don't force anything."

I did as he said.

"Good, now focus on every breathe," he said.

I did so.

"Focus on all the moving parts when you take each breathe."

I did so.

"Breathe."

I complied.

"Focus."

I complied.

"Breathe."

But my eyes gaped open.

"Nothing," I said.

Now his eyes widened. "No?" I quickly tried to downplay it, insisting I was ok, but his persistence knew no bounds. "Well don't feel bad," he said, "that's normal when you're just starting out."

"Oh yeah, it's f-

"Why don't you come back to the church with me, Naaj'?" I barely got a peep out before he continued. "If it's alright with you, I mean."

Whether intentional or not, he'd given me even less of a choice than the first go around.

"Yeah, I'll go," I blurted out.

He cheesed. "Well let's get back over there!"

But halfway down the exit, it occurred to me I had no idea what Isaiah even intended to do. "Watch your step," he said before I plopped down to the floor. "I'll be down in a minute."

I paced around the living room, trying to think of what he might have in mind or what difference going back to the church would make. "Ready?" Isaiah called, hardly a step down the stairs.

"Yeah," I replied as he impressively flew down the remainder. But my nerve was no greater, so I refrained from asking him a thing as we departed, and spent most of the ride back dodging any and all eye contact. "Believe me," he said, pulling up to the church, "it's gonna be alright."

I knew Isaiah could and *would* reinforce this a million times over until convinced I was feeling better, so I offered my false smile and nodded in agreement before leaping out of the van. But my huge head start occurred to me as I neared the church door while he hardly had a leg out of the drivers side.

"Go on in," he waved as I stood there, pretending not to hear until he caught up. As we passed the only occupied aisle inside, Isaiah graciously greeted the pair of men before leading me through a door off to the side of the stage. "Brothers?" he called. It took no time at all for his counterparts to come filing out of the adjacent kitchen, into the office area which I then realized had a desk for each of them plus Isaiah.

One reached for a handshake. "Have we met?" he asked, gripping my palm.

"This is Naaji, brothers," Isaiah stepped in. "He was one of our special guests earlier."

"Oh, that's right," he nodded. "Thought I recognized him. How are you?"

"Good," I said. Not one of their names stuck with me from the previous introduction so keeping interaction to a minimum would have been ideal, but, of course, the opposite was in store.

"He's here for bible study?" asked another 'brother'.

"Actually, I wanted to help him get into meditation," Isaiah replied.

All of their eyes lit up, but the one I shook hands with was first to speak. "C'mon, then," he said cheerfully.

But I was confused. Why were they all so keen on helping me? I could understand in Isaiah's case given our history, but the others were literal strangers with nothing to gain from it. Everyone had already gone home, so it wasn't as if they'd be putting on a show for the congregation. That said, the only remaining explanation was genuinely wanting to use their faith to help me which I couldn't help admiring. Each brother got into his position before signaling me toward my own, and I humbly obliged.

CHAPTER 6: A NEW BEGINNING

The grasp of Bari's slumber was finally relinquished after my rapid jabbing of his side with one hand and shaking of his shoulder with the other.

"What? I'm up, I'm up," he told me, glancing over at the clock.

"Why weren't you awake already? I thought you were going to set an alarm," I scolded.

"I did that, but it ain't wake me up. Why didn't you come make sure I was up earlier?"

"I was ready a while ago, so I was downstairs with Ivanna and her dad all this time. I didn't think you needed me to wake you up. Why are you so tired anyway?"

"They're ready to go?" asked Jabari.

"Yeah, just waiting on you."

"Well can you go down there and buy me some time?" Jabari asked.

"Yeah," I replied, exiting the room and closing its door behind myself.

Although Bari and I visited our house on numerous occasions and I received no calls from the Technological Enhancement Organization since the one nine months prior, I still felt forced into the same borderline shut-in boat as Bari as the uneasiness simply would not leave me. Fortunately for me however, he never questioned or seemed to mind staying away for so long anyway which I'd attributed to our practical inseparability leaving him content. Much of our time living with Ivanna and her dad was spent being exposed to both the bible and an immense faith in God which we soon became engrossed in ourselves.

Reaching the staircase which was in close vicinity to our room, I could hear chatter from downstairs, and each step closer to the bottom was accompanied by a gradual increase in its volume. It wasn't until one of my feet was planted on the livingrooms waxy wooden floor that I let go of the railing.

"Was he up already?!" called Ivanna before I could even reach the kitchen.

"He'll be ready in a minute," I declared, stepping in.

"Ok. You ready, Ivanna?" he asked.

"Yeah!" she said, insulted he even inquired.

"You better be," he said. "We have to go out there with confidence and show that we're learned in the scriptures." Despite being exposed to the bible for a large chunk of our time since moving in, Bari and I opted out of any part in debating with people who'd devoted anywhere near the same amount of time to their studies as Isaiah. "All the people being led astray by these groups need to know the truth. So just re-member what we went over, and stay away from topics you're not familiar with. They'll try to bait you into them, but if you avoid it, you'll be fine."

"I know, dad," she rolled her eyes.

"Good to hear," said Isaiah as his attention left her face and darted toward the kitchen door. "Good morning, Jabari."

"Morning," replied Bari. "Time to go?"

The three of us collectively confirmed this and we all got out of the kitchen. For this outing, I chose to wear a black t-shirt, cargo shorts, and sneakers that were meant more for style than comfort, forcing me to manipulate each step taken to avoid creasing them. Bari sported a maroon tank top showing off the toned physique he'd earned, grey shorts that only reached just above his knees, in addition to running shoes. Isaiah wore a collared shirt with 3 buttons down the chest, somewhat baggy jeans, and sandals which boasted his recently pedicured feet. Ivanna's hair was packed into a neat bun, and she had on a brownish orange blouse, white shorts, and flats.

As we walked one behind the other through the living-room, Ivanna grabbed her diminutive backpack and bible off of the couch and continued following closely behind Isaiah toward the front door. This made me consider if I'd forgotten something, and sure enough, I'd almost left my Extension behind.

I made a move for the stairs, but Ivanna immediately turned around asking, "Where ya going?"

"Getting my Extension. "I'll be outside in a sec," I said."

They proceeded outside while I raced up the staircase. I snatched it off the blowup and sealed the door on my way out. Upon opening the front door, I locked the bottom lock from inside of the house, and used my key to lock the top after closing it behind myself. Seeing Ivanna occupied the driver-side middle row seat, I looped around the vans rear, and entered through the opposite door.

"Everybody good?" asked Isaiah.

"Yeah," I replied.

"Mhm," Ivanna nodded.

"Yup," said Jabari.

Isaiah shifted the cars gears and backed out of his driveway. My attempt to then gaze out the window, however, was swiftly thwarted by Ivanna nudging my arm, prompting me to look her way.

"What's up?"

"Want some?" she asked, holding out a familiar bag.

Upon realizing its contents, I immediately nodded yes and dove into the bag.

"Wait, calm down," said Ivanna. "I didn't say the whole bag."

"Sorry," I replied, grabbing four worms in one hand, only to have them disappear into my mouth not a moment later. Their delectable fusion of sweet and sour rushed across my tastebuds.
"Jeez, Naaji."
"What?" I asked defensively. "You offered."
Jabari peered past his headrest to look at us.
"You guys take those worms way too seriously," he grinned. "They're nowhere near the best candy."

"Really!?" Ivanna barked. "Can you even name any candy that's better?"

Jabari thought for a moment. "Well," he said, "I *could* do that, but, the thing is, I don't want to bore you with such a long list."

Ivanna and I simultaneously scoffed in disgust.

"You two can keep telling yourselves that's the best candy out there if you want."

"You-"

"Forget it," I cut in. "He doesn't know what he's talking about."

"Clearly not," she replied, scarcely content.

Jabari wore an annoyingly smug expression as he refocused his attention on the road ahead.
My attempt at ignoring his ludicrous statement and reposition for a nap was cut off by the obnoxious sound of paper being rubbed together.

"Jeez!" I cried, looking at Ivanna. "What are you doing?

"I'm about to draw," she replied, flipping through the pages of her notepad.

"Oh yeah, I forgot it's Thursday."

"The heat's really getting to you, huh, Naaji?" asked Ivanna sarcastically.

"Better than last August's weather," I replied.

"Yeah, you're probably right," she agreed. "It was pretty bad last year."

My eyes left Ivanna's face to glance at some of her drawings as she leafed through the pad.

"Wait, what's that?" I asked, managing to catch a glimpse of one of her works of art.

The page flipping ceased, and Ivanna returned to the drawing she'd passed a moment prior.

"This one?"

"Yeah," I confirmed.

"It's a cocoon," she told me.

"Can I see?" I asked, holding my palm out.

"Sure." She handed the book over to me.

I scanned the page, saying, "This is really good."

"Think so?"

"Yeah," I replied, giving the notepad back. "When did you draw it?"

Ivanna thought momentarily before replying, "Some time in November."

"Mind if I take a look?" asked Jabari.

Ivanna reached forward with the notepad in hand, and he met her halfway.

"What're you going to draw today?" I asked.

"Not sure yet. I'm trying to think of something. You got any suggestions?"

"Well, since you drew a cocoon, why not draw a butterfly?"

Jabari turned and gave the notepad back to Ivanna.

"Good job," he told her.

"Thank you," she blushed.

Bari smiled and returned his attention to the road.

"What was it that you said I should draw?" asked Ivanna, looking my way.

"A butterfly."

"I just did that last week for like the fourth time," she said.

"I feel like you've already drawn most of what I'm going to think of, but how about a lamb?"

"Oh yeah, that's a good one," said Ivanna. "Thanks, Naaji."

"Sure," I said, repositioning myself for a nap. "Wake me up when we get there."

"Ok," she told me.

I then layed back on the headrest and fell asleep.

CHAPTER 7: FALSE PROPHETS

My eyes opened to Ivanna roughly hitting my shoulder.

"Ouch!" I exclaimed.

"We're here," she said.

I looked out the window and saw that we were on the highway in one of many lines of cars adjacent to one another, seeking entrance to New York via toll booths, and were up next in our respective line.

"No we're not," I replied. "I could still be asleep right now."

"The first camp isn't even far, so calm down!" Ivanna scolded.

"I didn't know; my bad."

Like every other state in the country, anyone entering and exiting New York was required, by law, to show their passport, have their vehicle searched by the person or, on rare occasions, the Strider, working the booth, and pay a small toll. This was one of three major national safety measures taken by the government in recent years(the other two being 5 foot barriers splitting the sidewalks of all major cities in the nation into lanes, strikingly similar to those in street's so that the constant traffic of pedestrians walking up and down streets can flow more fluently both in everyday life and during emergencies, as well as humongous walls hovering over every possible entrance and exit of the states for the protection of their citizens in the event of a lockdown-level emergency. After plenty of monthly state-wide lockdown drills back home in Jersey City, I understood that when the time for real ones arrived, the walls above whatever state or states in danger would be lowered to the ground, creating a fortress. Additionally, there would be plenty of sirens going off and voices from loud speakers instructing citizens on what to do. The toll booths we approached were identical to those I'd seen before in that they'd been placed inside of where the wall would stand if lowered, providing anyone working the booths shelter in the event of an emergency.

Isaiah pulled up to the booth for our turn.

"Hi, how are you?!" asked the man, working the booth.

"Good; and you?" replied Isaiah.

"I'm fine! Thank you!" The worker managed to somehow appear both exhausted and energized simultaneously. Ivanna, Bari and I handed our passports over to Isaiah who then gave it to the man who then checked to make sure they matched our faces followed by a surprisingly brief and laid back car search, ensuring we had no stowaways nor illegal items. "Seventy-five cents please," he said, sending Isaiah scrambling for change in his cupholder. Once he acquired the toll, he emptied it into the worker's outstretched hand. "Good to go, guys! Have a good one!" he said whilst tapping the vans roof.

"You too!" Isaiah replied, proceeding past the booth placing us directly into New York City where we ran into swiftly-moving traffic. I began blinking the subtle sleepiness from my eyes, allowing me to take in all the sights the city had to offer from diverse people going about their day, to towering skyscrapers that kissed the sky, to miscellaneous noise hammering my ears like no other placed I'd been.

"Right there!" shouted Bari, signaling Isaiah to the nearby corner where an uncharacteristically stationary crowd was.

"You sure?" asked Isaiah. "They weren't here in the videos."

"I guess they switched streets cause that's definitely them."

"Well now all we need is a parking spot," said Isaiah.

"Everybody look out for a spot," Bari told us.

I took a look at the camp and their decent-sized audience as we drove past.

"Turn at this corner," said Bari.

"Alright," replied Isaiah, bringing us to a one-way

street, narrowed by vehicles on either side, and very lightly peppered with open spaces throughout.

As Isaiah decelerated the car, Ivanna leaned forward. "Take that spot right there," she told him, holding on to his headrest with one hand and pointing with the other.

Isaiah cruised past five stationary cars and parallel parking behind what would have been the sixth. He pulled his key from the ignition, causing brief silence. "Let's get to it."

I climbed out of the car, and waited to regroup with the others on the sidewalk where I began limping in an attempt to stretch my legs.

"You good, Naaji?" asked Jabari, withdrawing from the automobile shortly after me.

"Yeah," I grunted, "my legs are just asleep."

Ivanna and Isaiah joined us.

"Everything alright?" asked Isaiah as I reached for my toes.

"Yeah, I'm ok," I replied, standing upright. "Let's go."

We walked the short distance from Isaiah's car to the corner, at which point, Bari said, "They're extra loud today."

"I know," replied Isaiah. "If you want, Ivanna, I can do this one."

"I'm fine," replied Ivanna.

"Alright," said Isaiah as we turned the corner and immediately became enveloped by people walking both toward and away from us. Upon struggling through this abundance of pedestrians, we reached our target, at which point I gazed over the heads of those within the crowd. There were 6 camp members total but before I could do anything more than glance at them all, my attention was captured by one who appeared to be in the midst of an argument with a red-haired woman whose face I couldn't see from where we stood. The camp member was bald with lightly tan skin, a thin nose that craned over at the tip. All six men wore purple robes with clearly artificial breast plates and gold patches both on their shoulders and around their waists.

But I could hardly make out what was being said in the shouting match before it came to an abrupt end as a loud pop assaulted my ears, followed closely by the man collapsing into a puddle of his own blood, and mobs of people scrambling in all directions.

"Run!" shouted Bari, running back around the corner we came from.
As we hurried down the block, I instantly regretted my choice of footwear, and, looking back, saw a metallic-blue Strider emerge from where we'd ran. Its left hand had morphed into a gatling gun. "Get down!" I squealed, yanking Jabari behind the nearest parked vehicle for cover. Ivanna dove alongside us while

Isaiah continued his race for the car. We followed after Isaiah in the street, using each passed car as cover.

"Hurry!" he shouted, climbing into the drivers seat.

To my surprise, while gun-fire was heard behind us, none of the bullets seemed to land anywhere near us, and, in about fifteen paces, we reached the van without a scratch.

"Go go go!" pleaded Bari once we got in. Isaiah did just that, and Ivanna swiftly scanned everyone for injuries.

"What just happened?" asked Isaiah.

"That Strider just glitched," I told him.

"Strider?"

"An android. The one we just saw was an Enforcer."

Isaiah looked confused.

"That's the model the police use," I added.

"Looked more like-"
Our Extensions made high pitched beeping sounds then a voice came from the speakers saying, "A member of the Hebrew Israelite Movement was gunned down on 45th Street, NYC just moments ago by a malfunctioning Strider, which officials headed to the scene say was likely glitched due to corrosion. More details on this breaking story will be posted on our

website later this evening. This has been Christine Miller from the New York sector of the United States News Conglomerate.

"We should g-" My arm suddenly began tingling while the veins branching through it simultaneously glowed blue.

"Your contact, Ivanna would like to telepathically communicate with you, said a voice in my head, negating all other sound around me. Would you like to communicate in this manner with him or her?"

I told the voice in my head yes, and soon heard Ivanna say, "Tell him what's really going on."

"What are you talking about?"
"Don't you think this might have to do with TEO?"
"Why would it?"
"Because a Strider just so happened to 'malfunction' and specifically shot at us after you pissed them off. It's time to tell him."
Ivanna's statement was spot-on, allowing for no conclusion to be reached, but one identical to hers.

"End call," I said out-loud, both returning my arm to normal and enabling me to hear outside of my thoughts.

"Everything alright?" asked Isaiah once the two of us were back to normal.

"Yeah, Naaji's just got somethin to tell Jabari."
"What?" asked Bari.

"Someone from TEO threatened me. That's why I wanted to leave home."

"What did you do?"

"What did *I* do?" I asked

"For them to threaten you," he added.

"I didn't think we were ready to sign a contract with them at the time, so I turned it down."

"And now we think they were controlling the Strider that attacked us," Ivanna interjected.

"And I think you're right," said Bari.

"Why!?" I asked.

"Cause you pissed off the most powerful technology company in the world. And there's a whole lot more to them than people see."

"Like what?" asked Isaiah.

"Well, for one, 'TEO' actually stands for, 'The Enlightened Ones'. Whole thing's a front for a secret society."

My eyes widened. "What kind of secret society?"

"The worst kind. And nobody tells them no, so that explains why things got so crazy when you turned them down."

"Why do you know all this stuff?"

"Dad told me in case something like this happened. Actually, no, he told me so something like this *wouldn't* happen."

I wondered to myself why my dad would keep these things from me, and tell Bari, but getting out of danger was far more important in that moment. "Lets go back to the house."

"Cant do that. What if they follow us? Then they know where we've been hiding."

"So what do we do, then?"

Bari grabbed the GPS from the dashboard. "We're going to Durai."

"You mean Dubai?" asked Isaiah.

"Nah that's a guy our dad always talked about. I think he can help us."

"Where is he?"

"He owns a hotel not that far from here," he said returning the GPS to its previous position. Isaiah re-adjusted as it began providing directions, and we were on our way.

CHAPTER 8: HELP WANTED

Before we entered, I looked up at the hotel's name, Garvish Tower, in grand letters as the sun reflected off of it. People inhabiting the lobby were busy going about their business, allowing us to go straight to the front desk where multiple workers were stationed. The woman we walked up to had multiple layers of makeup smothering her face, a perimeter of darkness around her constantly fanning eyes which showed off extended lashes, crimson lipstick, straightened black hair as well as an all black uniform dress equipped with a metal nametag I was too distracted to read on account of everything else she had going on.

"Can we please speak to Mr. Garvish?" asked Jabari.

"Is everything alright, sir?"

"Yes. Can we just please see him?"

"One second, sir; I'll see if he's available," she replied, unhooking the nearby telephone, dialing a number, and awaiting an answer before once again speaking.

"Good afternoon, Mr. Garvish, a few people are here to see you." She briefly paused. "What are your names?" We introduced ourselves and she recited our names followed by another pause. "Ok, sir, be right there." She hung up and came from behind the desk to lead us to an employee only hallway that was dimly lit. Before leaving us to return to her post, she pointed straight ahead saying, "Through that door down there."

Bari walked ahead the entire way and entered the office that didn't have much to it where a man greeted us. "Welcome to my establishment."

"Hey, Durai," said Bari.

He had purple eyes that were clearly the product of contacts, a grey- haired comb over, tan skin, a small bridged nose with a wide tip, a broad body, and, oddly enough, informal black shorts and t-shirt. "I think proper introductions are in order. What were your names again?" he asked Isaiah and Ivanna.

"Pleasure's mine. What brings you by?"

"I think Naaji might be in trouble with The Enlightened Ones."

"What for!?"

"Did you hear about the Hebrew Israelite that got shot?"

"Yeah, I heard the news broadcast. Why?"

"We were there when the Strider supposedly malfunctioned and shot him. "And then it came after us," Ivanna added.

"But why would they be after Naaji?' asked Durai.

"Because I didn't think we were ready to sign a contract with them yet and then they threatened me."

He scratched his chin in contemplation. "Its definitely a strong possibility. You told them no, they threatened you, and now a Strider, they could easily have taken control of, just killed a guy right in front of you and then went after you."

"That's what *I* said," bragged Ivanna.

Durai faced me. "Did you ever show them your face?"

"They did a video call interview with me once."

His face grew grim. "So it's not that much of a stretch to say TEO took a picture of his face when they video called and the Strider recognized him today. They could've been controlling it remotely too."

"But what's the point of the secret society though?" asked Isaiah. "What do they even want?"

"The entire society gets orders from its 1st Echelon members, and they're divided through different headquarters like the one here in New York," he said. "What they want in general is control over the world using all the potential weapons of mass destruction they can find and fund."

"Hm. But why'd they kill the other guy?" asked Isaiah.

"I guess it was more of a warning shot to show they're serious."

"So what do we do now?"

"Its time for you to meet with TEO, Naaji."

Ivanna and Jabari simultaneously disagreed, and so did I. "I'm not doing that! They wanna kill me!" I cried.

"You're not in a ditch somewhere right now, so clearly they still see use in you. Just go settle on a deal with them, and all of this can stop. Nobody else needs to get hurt."

"So you expect me join a secret society that wants world domination?" I asked.

"No, I expect you to gain their trust and work your way up the ranks. You can stop them from the inside."

"There's gotta be a safer option than that," Bari frowned.

"Like what?"

"I don't know," replied Bari. "Anything but that."

"Look; why don't you guys just take some time to relax and at least consider it."

"Alright," I said with no intent at changing my mind.

"Go get the keys to room 1035 at the front desk. I'll tell them I sent you," he told us.

"Ok."

We left his office and walked the short path back to the lobby. One of the women at the desk gave us what we sought without even being asked. "Enjoy your stay!" she said with a smile.

We went over to be nearby elevators where three people, whom appeared to be together, were waiting.

"You're not doing what he said, Naaji."

"I know; he's crazy," I replied. "I thought you said he could help."

"He can. We just need a better plan."

"Well we better think fast before they find us again," Isaiah said.

The elevator doors opened and we made way for people exiting before inserting ourselves behind the group ahead of us. Their bags made it a bit of a tight squeeze but we managed.

One of the three elderly women gently poked my shoulder. "Could you hit nine for me please?"

"Sure," I obliged after hitting our own floors number.

The elevator took no time at all to reach their floor. "Excuse us," said one of them. We stepped aside, they exited, and just as soon as the doors closed, they re-opened on our floor. I checked the plaques showing which rooms lied down the right and left paths. "This way," I said, choosing the latter. Room numbers rose in order, switching from the left and right sides of the hall as we speed walked down.

"Whats the room again?" I asked.

"1035," replied Isaiah, prompting me to stop two doors down. I put the key card in the door and it unlocked with an oddly satisfying sound allowing us to enter.

The room featured a bathroom near the door, one neatly made bed with nightstands on either side, a desk below the TV hanging on the wall, and a couch next to the window outlooking the city.

"What are we gonna do about this?" Ivanna asked once everyone took a seat on the bed.

Isaiah spoke up. "Why don't you call the police?"

"The evidence is gone anyway so-"

Multiple bangs on the door startled us. "NYPD! Open up!"

Nobody moved and three more bangs thudded against the door. "NYPD! We know you're in there!"

I was too confused to do anything.

"Open it up," I heard a voice say before the door

opened and four officers rushed in.

"On the ground now!" shouted the bald one, forcing me to the floor by my shoulder and cuffing me in unison with the others on Ivanna, Jabari, and Isaiah.

"What's going on!?" I squirmed.

"Stop resisting! You're all under arrest!"

"We didn't do anything!" cried Ivanna.

"Ouch!" Isaiah squealed.

"Under arrest for what!?" asked Bari.

"Lets hurry this up, I'm ready to go on break!" the officer told his partners after lifting me to my feet.

Durai stepped into the doorway.

"The hell's going on, man!?" I asked.

"Just make this easier on everybody and stop resisting," he told me.

"Thanks for the tip," said the officer as we passed Durai.

"Have a good one, Herb," he replied.

"You too, Mr. Garvish."

CHAPTER 9: CAN'T DO THE TIME...

When we arrived at the police station, scents from an absurd amount of odor-killing products flew up my nose. But I assumed it was for the best as to fight off the clashing stench of whatever scum came through the doors. The very same officer Durai exchanged words with back at the hotel led us straight past rows of neatly arranged desks, some occupied by lone workers, others with the addition of what seemed to be arrestees across from them. I was on edge as it was, and being brought to a dead-silent hallway didn't help.

"Don't move," ordered the officer before whispering into a nearby room. He quickly retracted his head and stared right at me. "Lets go."

I looked around as if not knowing whom he spoke to, but this only ticked him off to the point of snatching me from where I stood. In the room awaited a man seated at his desk.

"How are you?" he asked with a perplexingly genuine

tone.

"I'll be better when somebody explains what's going on," I replied. "We didn't do anything."

"And I haven't even accused you of anything," he said calmly. "But anyway, let's start over. I'm Detective Stokes and you are...?"

"Naaji Busara."

He reached between his computer monitor and printer to shake my hand. "Well, first of all, Naaji, you're not in any trouble as long as you just hand it over."

"Hand what over?" I asked only to receive a booming slap to the back of my head, courtesy of the officer. The hell's your problem!?"

"Jesus, Herb!" scolded Detective Stokes. "Take a walk!"

I nursed the point of impact as Officer Herb slammed the door behind him.

"You ok?"

What do you think? I thought to myself. "Yeah, I'm alright, but I *really* don't know why we're here."

"Because we'll be taking your inventions off your hands, Naaji," he said simply.

This felt all too familiar and I instantly knew our previous problem had resurfaced to plague us once again, this time at the hands of police. Or were they in on it with TEO all along? Chuckling uneasily, I replied, "They're actually not for sale."

"Well I'm sorry, Naaji, but 'No,' isn't an option. So I advise you not to be difficult with us cause then I'd have to call the Chief, get him involved, and you definitely don't want that; trust me. Just tell me where you've got the stuff. Help me help you."

"What do you want with our inventions anyways?" I asked.

"I'm not at liberty to tell you that. Just know, cooperating with us is the smartest option right now." He stared at me, anticipating a response while I stared right back, trying to think of one. With his beardless face and hairless head, Detective Stokes appeared, at the very least, to be in his early or mid-thirties. Though I couldn't see the outfits lower half, he seemed well put together based on the coordination between his tie and wrinkleless button-down.

"We're not giving up our stuff without a good reason," I said firmly.

"Hardball it is."

In a blur, Detective Stokes snatched my hand to his side of the desk and revealed a small black-screened pad. He forcibly pressed my thumb onto it, let go after about ten seconds, and typed away on his computer.

"What're you doing?"

"Putting our latest convict in the system."

"Convict?! But I-"

"Shut up!" There wasn't a grain of good will left in Detective Stokes' now glaring eyes. "Get up!" he ordered, blasting to his feet. Before I knew it, he'd shoved me back into the hallway where Officer Herb and the others were nowhere to be found.

"Where'd they go?"

"Keep walking!" he pushed. I could feel my heart and chest thumping against one another with each step, taking us further and further down the hall. At the end lied a door which Detective Stokes shewed me aside to unlock, and on the other side were aisles of tall filing cabinets, no doubt loaded with items. "Straight ahead," he said, only to place a deathgrip on my arm, and yank me down the aisle aligned with the doorway. A locked panel was amongst floor tiles near the wall exactly opposite to where we'd come in. Wherever I was being taken, it definitely wasn't good, and nothing but bad presumptions bounced around my head. But we'd clearly passed the point of asking questions, so my anxiety wouldn't be alleviated. Once open, I carefully descended into the panel step by step with only minimal light from whatever space I was entering as aid. Detective Stokes manhandled me into a wooden chair at the rooms center, directly beneath a single flickering light fixture and restrained my hands with belt-like clamps on both arms of the chair. "You made this a whole lot harder than it needed to be."

He pulled out a small cylinder-shaped device, and flared his arm out, extending it into a baton. But just when I thought a simple beating was in order, the first bit of contact vaulted me into a state, alternating between numbness and immense pain. Jolts of electricity ran up and down my body with each subsequent press of the baton against my chest. I strained, best I could, in an effort to brace for impact as he tortured me with shock after shock. My eyes reeled back and forth, becoming blurred by tears of anguish. Every second dragged along at a snail's pace and all I could wonder was, *Why.* Not, *Why is this happening,* or, *Why me,* but, *Why aren't I dead already.* The pain went on and on until he decided I'd had enough and let me loose. I practically had to be carried back up the stairs and to the hallway before my legs stopped buckling under me.

"I hope you understand how serious we are now," he smirked in satisfaction. After being led back to the front of the station, I asked where he was taking me. But a verbal response was unnecessary as a set of nearby doors brought us to a hall lined with holding cells, left and right. As we walked through, I tried to avoid eye contact but couldn't help myself. It was a relief that none of the detainee's seemed to be unhinged.

"Here you go," said Detective Stokes as we stopped right in front of the cell where the others were being held. I must have looked just as bad as I felt judging by Ivanna's immediate reaction.

"The hell did you do to him!?" she roared. "Where's the police chief? I want to talk to him."

Stokes unlocked the cell and tossed me, stumbling in. "I *am* the chief of police. I'll let you talk things over and then I'm coming back for your turn," he hissed before walking away.

Bari's eyes dampened as he watched Ivanna and her dad sit me up. "What did he do to you?" she asked in a slightly more tame tone.

"He kept shocking me," I shivered.

"That guys an asshole!"

Yea no shit, I thought. "He's crazy."

"Yeah, and he thinks he's gonna come back for me, like I won't kick his ass." The look on Ivanna's face was instantly recognizable; She clearly meant business, but even still, Stokes had proven he wasn't one to be trifled with either. "I mean, who does he think he is? I swear-"

"You gotta calm down, hun'," Isaiah told her. "I know you're upset, but we have to be smart. I'm sure what the Chief of Police is doing can't be legal, so let's just report him."

"But we're stuck here," I groaned, shaking off the last of the tingles. "And plus they're all in on this together."

"Who is?"

"TEO and the police," said Bari. "They've got crazy connections all over."

"Yeah, and clearly your friend from the hotel's one of them," Ivanna chimed in.

"Sorry. I mean, I thought we could trust him for sure. But what did he say to you anyway, Naaji?"

"Same as what the guy on the phone said: he wants our inventions."

"Well why don't you just give them up then?" asked Ivanna.

"No!"

"Well I guess we'll just stay here forever then, right?" she fired back.

"Guess so!" I shrugged.

"But if that's all they want, why not give it to them so we can leave?" Isaiah asked.

"We didn't bust our asses all those hours just to hand

our stuff over."

Bari panted. "I don't think there's any other way. We've seen what they're willing to do."

"It doesn't-

Out of nowhere, our cell door swung open and I tried to race out, but got knocked back at the doorway. There wasn't anything there though.

"You alright, Naaj'?!" asked Isaiah.

"Shhhhh," said a bodiless female voice.

Bari hugged the wall, asking who was there.

"Just calm down; I'm getting you out of here," whispered the voice.

I felt something latch onto my chest and looked down to see a circular metal device with a small panel of buttons that soon vanished along with my body and clothing.

"AH!" I yelped.

"What just happened to him!?" asked a wide-eyed Isaiah.

"Shush!" the voice demanded once again.

"The hell's happening?" I said.

"Look, I'm Durai's partner," she said. "I'm here to help, but you're all going to have to shut up and do what I say." Even with everything that transpired following our arrival at the hotel, no one questioned the invisible woman as she subjected them to the same cloak as I. "Now hold hands and walk in a line." It took some blind feeling around, but we managed to follow this order before she led us out of our enclosure. This time, I didn't allow other arrestees to draw my attention while we passed, as any misstep could ruin our lines flow, drawing someone's attention. The space crowded with desks and people surprisingly wasn't all that treacherous minus having to dodge Stokes as he marched towards the holding area.

When we made it to the front of the building, I asked, "What now?"

"Just stay close," replied the woman, yanking us to a side street around the corner where a double parked SUV awaited. "Right there."

The tinted driver side window rolled down and revealed Durai. "Get in!" he called.

But all of our attention was immediately drawn to the woman as her cloak dispersed, allowing low cut curls, pale ivory skin, and baggy cargo pants with a compression shirt to be seen. "Push the middle button on the cloaks I stuck to you," said the woman.

I, along with the others, did so, causing our cloaks to diminish before we filed into the SUV.

Durai jammed the accelerator asking, "I told you guys I'm in TEO right?"

"No!" Ivanna barked before I had the chance to.

"I know you're probably mad but-"

"No shit we're mad, you sold us out for no reason!"

"If you shut up and listen, he'll explain what happened," replied Durai's partner.

Right away, I knew she'd messed up talking to Ivanna, like that. You couldn't get away with saying anything remotely slick to her on a good day, much less when she was annoyed. " 'cuse me?"

I considered intervening but thought better of it. "Not helping, Molly," said Durai with a deep breath.

"But like I was saying, you have every right to be mad, but I wouldn't have done what I did for no good reason."

"Well why'd you do it?" I asked. "We could've died in there!"

"Not likely," he scoffed. "They try to get as much out of you as possible first. And I only did it so I could get promoted."

"Promoted?" asked Bari.

"Yeah, to a higher Echelon, so I could find out more about their plans.

But being his unknowing pawn didn't sit well with me. "You could've said something instead of just using us like that," I told him.

"Right," Ivanna agreed.

"Yeah, I get that and I'm sorry."

He sounded genuine and, after all, he *had* just saved us. While none of us verbally acknowledged it, the peaceful silence that filled the car worked well enough.

"How'd you end up getting in TEO anyway?" Bari finally spoke up.

"They didn't force me if that's what you're wondering; I wanted to join because I knew how far they could take me and my work. And the money to open my hotel was a plus.

"What inventions did you make so far?" I asked.

"Just one. My contracts almost up, and I'm supposed to turn in my long range EMP soon. That's not happening though."

After everything we learned they were capable of

since the initial phone call, I completely understood Durai wanting to keep what was his out of TEO hands.

"Won't they come after you too then?" asked Isaiah.

"They definitely will, and that's where you all come in. We can put our heads together and get them before they get us."

We stared blankly at one another, considering the offer.

"Look, I *really* need your help. I wouldn't be asking if I didn't," he added.

"He sure does, cause those slobs he hired won't be any help," said his partner.

"Molly, they're inventors. They didn't sign up to risk their lives."

"What for then? Just to sit in the lab and get over-paid?"

"Anyway," replied Durai, "since TEO have police connections, you'll never know who to trust, so that leaves you two options: you can either run from them for the rest of your lives which is pretty impossible with all their assets; or you can help us fight back." He looked at the four of us crunched up in the backseat. "What's it gonna be?"

"I don't think-"

"Don't you want to get back at them for your dad?"

"What are you talking about?" I asked.

"That plane crash wasn't an accident, they killed him. I know they did."

I eyed Bari. "Why would they?"

"Look, he probably never told you this, but your dad was stressed out all the time about making another big invention for TEO. But one day, he actually told me what happens to the people they don't need anymore. And then a week later I hear about his private jet crashing in a 'freak accident'? I'm not buying it."

Before Bari or I could reply Isaiah said, "He's right. If your dad was a part of this society, and they're as wicked as you guys say, it's not that crazy of jump."

"And who knows how many others they've gotten rid of?" said Durai.

I found it impossible to ignore the things that were now clear as day. It wasn't just about my parents either. Countless lives were at stake, and we couldn't just do nothing, knowing what we now knew."

"You're right, but how are we even supposed to get to them if they're such a big deal?" I asked.

"Well, I know where to find them, we just need a plan is all.

Bari took a deep breath. "So I guess we're doing this."

"Yup," replied Ivanna.

Durai was clearly ecstatic. "Alright!" he said, glancing back at us. "Oh, and what did you two invent again?"

"Electromagnetic Stasis Grenades, and Electric Discharge Pistols," I replied. "Should we get em?"

"Anything helps. Where are they?"

I pointed towards Ivanna and Isaiah who both were to my left. "We left them at their house."

"They live far?"

"Bayonne, New Jersey." I noticed a black plate-like device with a red and green light on it. "What's that black thing?"

"That's my EMP. I brought it just incase, but Molly

swiped a guard's cell key."

"We could probably use that too," I said.

"Yeah, I figured we would. The cloaks too; and the other stuff they made back at the hotel. Oh, and do you know anything about an Accessible Strider?"

"Huh?"

"Your dad told me about it: It looks just like a regular Strider, except you can actually get in it. Said he kept it in the house.

"Our basements the only thing he could be talking about. And we live close to them anyway."

"Alright, well lets go right now. If it works like he said, I can probably program it to look like one of the 1st Echelon members," he said, only to strangely pull over right after.

"What's up?" I asked.

No answer.

Looking over at him, Molly said, "He answered a call." It was then that I leaned forward to see blue streaks of light ranging from his Extension to his head confirming this.

About a minute of awkward silence went by and Durai came back to us. "We gotta go back to the hotel."

"Why?"

"TEO sounds suspicious. They'll probably be sending someone to come check up on me at the hotel, so I gotta hide you. We're heading back over there for a bit."

CHAPTER 10:
DREAM TEAM

F our people, each sitting at scrap-riddled tables of their own, glanced up from their work, and the only woman amongst them sprung from her seat. "How'd my cloaks do?" she asked with a nas-ally voice.

"They did good, but I gotta go handle something. Introduce yourselves guys," said Durai, making his exit from the lab.

All four inventors left their posts to approach us. "I'm Kayla," said the woman, "and this is Pramin, Rian, and Mustapha."

"What's up?"

"Hey."

"Sup?"

Pramin had blue eyes, prickly black hair enveloped in gel causing it to glisten, a nose pinched together from both sides, broad body, and a full grown beard that could somewhat compete with Jabari's. Mustapha's hair was almost identical to mine, and his nose was flattened to a wideness. Rian, on the other hand, had a mustache, hightop fade, circular-lensed glasses, and pointed fleshy nose. Kayla had beautiful long dreads in a neat ponytail, and a short chubby nose. All four of them wore khakis with tucked in black uniform shirts sporting the hotel's name across the chest.

"Hey you wanna check out my laser pointer?" asked Pramin, returning to his table.

"Sure," I replied.

He placed an apple on the floor. "Watch this." Pramin proceeded to turn on the silver pin-like gadgets red laser and point it at the apple, taking no time to neatly split it in half. "Pretty cool, right?" he smiled.

"Yeah!" I replied.

"We'll go next," said Mustapha, wrapping his arm around Rian. On one of their tables sat a watch that Mustapha grabbed and put on. He fiddled with it for a moment, causing a chrome black material to spread across his upper body, stopping at his neck.

"Is it armor?" Bari asked.

"Yup, exo armor. Lets go, Rian."

To all of our surprise, Rian picked up a pistol from the table, paced back, and shot Mustapha in the chest five times, neglecting to let us shield our ears. The bullets bounced off of the smooth surface shielding Mustapha. I shook the jarring echo of gunfire from my ears. "That's cool too, but can't they hear the gun upstairs?"

"Nah, the walls are way too thick to hear through."

Isaiah requested to hear his name again, and Mustapha told him, adding that he was fine being called

"Mu" as well.

The door creaked open. "I'm back!" said Durai.

"Everything alright?" asked Isaiah.

"Yeah, it should be. They sent somebody to check up on me, but it's handled, so we can go get everything we need."

"Should I come too?" asked Molly.

"Nah, I think we'll be alright." He turned to his inventors. "You should start brainstorming ideas for a plan."

"Alright," said Kayla as we made our exit behind Durai.

CHAPTER 11:
HOME SOMEWHAT
SWEET HOME

Nothing at all seemed to have changed from our last visit home aside from the once rich scent of pine cone becoming much less potent. But this was expected without us there to activate the movement-triggered air fresheners. Beyond this, I found comfort in the fact that there were no signs of TEO paying a visit in our absence. However, I didn't wish to stay any longer than necessary. Bari and I went right over to the basement door, opened it, flicked on the light, and went downstairs. Our dad's Mark 1 Strider stood dead center in the room by his work table where I last saw it.

"Beautiful," said Durai from the bottom step. It was an inch or two taller than me and, despite feeling hollow, was still no joke to carry alone. I arched my back whilst hugging the stiff figure to prevent it from sliding out of my grasp. "Help me get it upstairs," I told Bari, prompting Durai to move out of the way.

"I gotchu," he replied, grabbing the legs. "You go infront." Bari pushed as I pulled the Strider, being careful not to trip while backing my way up.

There was a silent moment of triumph as we looked at one another upon making it to the top where the others waited.

"I got the door," said Isaiah, making way for us.

"Need help?" asked Ivanna before I waved her off.

"Nah we got it."

Isaiah shut the door behind us once we lugged the Strider out, and Ivanna opened the trunk for us to place it at a perfect angle before shutting it back and getting in the back seat.

"Bayonne next, right?" asked Durai.

"Yeah," Isaiah replied, climbing into the passenger seat.

"What's the address?"

"12 Stevenson."

Durai punched this into his GPS before pulling off, and I rested my leg against the door as we rumbled down the beat up street, straight to a red light. In the car next to us was an older man smoking a cigarette with his window down. He happily danced to whatever song was being played on the radio and I turned to see if anybody else noticed. But Ivanna looked straight ahead and Bari stared off while rapidly tapping his heel. Everyone seemed to be in their own zone, so I didn't stray from mine. The light flashed green and, again, we were off.

With minimal traffic, it only took a few minutes to reach our next stop. Unbuckling my seatbelt, I said, "Be right back," and after reaching the front door, pulled out my keys to let myself in. Even without an inhabitants, their house managed to feel more welcoming than ours. I went right upstairs to our room, retrieving the bag with our four ESGs and two EDPs out of the closet before returning downstairs and out of the house, locking the door behind myself.

But the others were nowhere to be found, and a new visitor had arrived in their stead: a Strider staring me down, guns at the ready.

"Move!" yelled Ivanna from my left. With their attention momentarily taken, I vaulted over the railing, dumping everything out of the bag for us to defend ourselves. While her dad wanted no part of it, Ivanna jumped to action. She and Durai mimicked Bari and I, tossing a third and fourth ESG after ours, alas, no gunfire came in return, so we stood ready to fire our EDP's as well.

"You get it?" Isaiah peeked. But the lone strider had disappeared, and sticking around to search for it wasn't in our best interest.

"We gotta go." I led the charge back to the vehicle, scooping our gadgets along the way.

"That's everything, right?" asked Durai. I investigated the backpack before nodding. "Let's head back."

CHAPTER 12: PRACTICE MAKES BETTER

My arms and hands ached with pain as Bari and I carried the Strider into the inventors lab which access to was exclusive to those with the elevator key to its floor. There was nothing but happiness in my body once we stood it up as gently as we could on the floor.

"What's up with the Strider?" asked Kayla. "I'm gonna program it to look like somebody from the 1st Echelon," Durai smirked as he got right to work on it. "So what plan did you guys think of?"

"A really simple one," she said. "Use my cloaks to sneak in, and then use everything we've got to take out security and get to the 1st Echelon."

I gulped. "Is that it?"

"Um, pretty much. Oh and you've got the Strider too, so that helps."

Sensing our skepticism building, Durai said, "Yup, plus we got my EMP and Naaji and Jabari's stuff."

"And I'm guessing these four are just gonna sit this

one out and wait for their checks, right?" asked Molly, staring Kayla down.

"Anyway, that's the plan. What do you think?"

"I don't think we really have a choice," said Bari.

Durai was still working away, so I decided to test out our own inventions while I had the chance. "You got any more of those apples?" I asked Rian.

"Yeah, right in that basket over there," he pointed. "Why? You got something to test?"

I grabbed an apple from the basket, placed it on the floor a good distance from everyone, and pulled out all four ESGs and both EDPs from the backpack. "Watch this." I cranked one of the ESGs knobs all the way to the right, indicating I wanted the largest possible bubble to be produced upon detonation which was five seconds away according to the digital countdown which then appeared. Soon after I tossed it, the apple was lifted off the floor into a vibrant bubble of energy. I heard the others, including Molly, gasp in awe up until the bubble popped sending faint particles of energy in all directions and the apple to the floor with a thud.

"How long did it take you guys to make that?" asked Mu.

"Some years," replied Bari, bathing in the recognition. I tested out the remaining ESGs with the same result and moved on to the EDPs which constantly generated energy to blast using a perpetual chemical reaction within the clip. I pulled the trigger, sending a ball of sparks at the apple, burning it to a crisp followed by a second shot with the other EDP to finish it off.

Before anyone could compliment us on this invention as well,

Durai said, "Got it!" attracting all of our attention.

"Its ready?" I asked.

"I'm pretty sure. Lets see," he said, fiddling inside the open slot behind the Striders neck until its head abruptly took the form of a bald, sleepy-eyed, elderly man with a heavily protruding nose, seemingly sculpted for the sole purpose of allowing its user to look down upon others from the apex. He then grabbed a red, hooded robe with an emblem of two palms(one over the other) and a sphere between them in the chests center. The robes bottom reached the floor. "The robes a copy of the ones the 1st Echelon wears."

"Who's face is that?"

"Nobody but the 1st Echelon knows each other's names. I just snuck this picture at one of their events," said Durai.

"So, we're good to go, right?" I asked.

"Actually, I'd rather you two get some real practice with your inventions first."

"How?"

Durai, turning to Molly, said, "You mind?"

She stopped skeptically scanning the inventors. "Yeah, come on," she told us. Bari and I each grabbed one EDP and an ESG before going after her. Isaiah and Ivanna tried to follow, but she waved them off. "Just these two."

Surprisingly, Ivanna didn't retort and Molly brought

us to the other side of the room where another elevator awaited, the doors of which opening for us in no time. There were only a few options on this one's panel, but I couldn't quite make out what they said with my crummy eyesight and all. Under other circumstances I'd probably have said something-anything to break the ice, but Molly's body language didn't exactly scream, *Speak to me*, so I bit my tongue and focused on the queasy feeling instilled by the elevator as we made our descent. Once the doors opened she charged out, going right, as walls were both ahead and to the left. A sign which read, *Recreational Center*, connected our paths two sides. I glanced into each set of windowed double doors we passed, all of which to our right, and found a basketball court, track, swimming pool, a paintball course-resembling space, and finally, our destination: a shooting range. There were five lanes and Molly scanned her hand on a panel next to the first, opening racks with guns and ammo below each of them.

"Alright, gimme a second; I just need a warmup," she said. Bari and I stood back when she chose, then loaded a pistol of her liking. Three shots were quickly fired, all crashing not only into the life-sized targets head, but my eardrums twofold. Once she depleted the remaining bullets in the clip, Molly turned to us. "Wanna shoot?"

I immediately refused, but, for some reason, Bari went right up to a lane of his own for a turn. He loaded and began firing the gun of his choosing before she could even offer assistance-not that she would've anyway.

"You might as well try too," Molly told me.

I waved the EDP in my hand. "All we're using is these."

"You should still know how to shoot a *real* gun."

This irked me more than it probably should have. What did she know? Why would we resort to such a barbaric route with a non-lethal option that was just as efficient at our disposal? Why would she assume I couldn't shoot a gun? Regardless of how nonsensical this all seemed, it was now my mission to make Molly eat her words. Of course, it would have helped to have had any form of prior experience handling firearms. I immediately made a fool of myself, trying to choose a gun and its appropriate ammo.

"Take from whatever's right under the gun you want," Molly groaned impatiently.

But I ignored her, carrying on as if I already knew. With one eye shut, and the gun aimed at my target, I pulled the trigger. However, much to my bewilderment, both the bullet and booming sound I braced for failed to reveal themselves.

"It's on safety," she said, coming over to me.

I quickly tried to correct the issue on my own and shoot, but still nothing.

"Give it here," Molly snatched. I heard something click and she gave it right back to me. "Go ahead."

Once again, I shut my left eye, and squinted the other, focusing on the target ahead. As I held it, the pistol actually had a lighter feel than our EDP's, but shooting it made me jerk back and slightly fumble it in my hands. The mission was accomplished though. *I hit it!*

I thought to myself, admiring the dent my shot left.

"You were standing wrong," Molly pointed out.

"How?"

She tapped the back of my foot forward until it was a decent distance from the other. "Keep your shoulders square too. And just shoot."

I adjusted myself accordingly and sent another bullet slamming against the target. It admittedly felt much better to shoot following the adjustments.

"Thanks," I mumbled.

"Sure," she said. Just go ahead and finish, so we can go."

Assuming a cryptic reply was in store, I didn't bother asking her to elaborate, but instead continued shooting until my last bullet met its target. When I turned to Molly with a, *What now?*, *look,* she said to put the safety back on, so I squinted, felt around and eventually did, putting my weapon of choice back in its place afterwards. We made our exit from the shooting range and entered a previously passed room down the hall.

"Looks like a paintball course," I say.

"Yeah," Bari agreed.

There were concrete barriers all over the room with the additions of dirt hills and ramps, providing higher ground while lights hung above to shine throughout.

"You two, go over there," pointed Molly before marching the opposite way. But Bari and I hardly got anywhere when a bullet whizzed by, it's momentous wind grazing my arm. I spun around, demanding an explanation for this. "That's the only freebie you're getting, so you better be ready," she said. Before I could scold any further, the gun was raised in our direction once again, so I dove to cover alongside Bari.

"What's she doing?!" Bari cried, clearly shaken up.

"What's your problem!" I shouted.

"Don't you need practice?"

"Yeah, but–

"Then let's go!" she fired back. A lone bullet struck our barrier.

"What do we do?" Bari shuttered.

We had to fight back. That was the only answer. I quickly peeked out and saw Molly approaching methodically. "Alright, listen," I whispered, "we're gonna split up; you stay low, I'll go high. All you have to do is distract her and I got the rest."

Bari's split of our gadgets shook in his rattling hands, but he gave a nod of agreement.

"Go!" I sprung up. She fired two more shots, but I reached the nearest ramp. More shots followed. I heard a surge of electricity build and slam against something. It was Bari. He'd fired his EDP, and Molly instead began unloading on his cover. I checked how far she was from my vantage point, before activating my ESG's timer. While their exchange continued, I tossed it down at her and she was sprung into its bubble almost instantly.

"Yeah!" I cheered, stumbling back down the ramp. "Alright, let me down," she ordered.

"Are you gonna try to kill us again?" I mocked, receiving no reply.

Bari resealed the ESG and Molly landed on her hands

and knees.

"Pretty good," she said begrudgingly. The journey back upstairs was a blur as I replayed our victory in my head. At the lab, the others still went about their business while Bari and I watched closely. Ivanna and her dad looked on too, but it was obvious they didn't appreciate it as much. For me, however, it reached a point where I began to stare blankly at their work.

"Hey, Naaji," said Pramin, brushing sweat from his head, "you good?"

"Yeah, why?"

"I don't know, you look a little out of it."

I wasn't sure how to take this. I felt as fine as a situation like this allowed, especially with the way Bari and I had just conducted ourselves in the standoff with Molly. "Nah, I'm good, just thinking."

"Well, if you're bored I'm going to the pool if you wanna come." Considering everything at stake, I couldn't wrap my head around his nonchalant attitude, but then again, doing something aside from fighting for our lives was a welcome change.

"Sure," I shrugged.

"Here." He handed me a rectangular touchpad. "Order some swim trunks. Anybody else coming?" he asked a disinterested crowd.

The device's interface was made specifically for Durai's establishment, sporting sliding photos of all things it offered as well as tabs for accessing them. I pressed the one named, *Clothing,* which opened a dropdown menu with more options for me to browse until finding, *Male Swimwear.*

"Just get one," he told me.

Once I clicked my desired item, it brought me to a page detailing it, followed by another which read, *Purchase Confirmed! Thank You!*

"Did it," I said.

"They'll send them up in a minute," Pramin assured.

Not long after, my pair of trunks *did* in fact arrive via tube near the labs entry elevator. I retrieved them and we went down to the recreational floors pool where Pramin jumped straight in, splashing water at my feet.

"You can swim, right?"

"Yeah," I replied.

"Well you can change in the locker room over there," he pointed.

I dodged the spilled pool water and lounge chairs to go change. The single aisle of lockers and a long bench were placed out of sight of the doorless entrance. I frantically undressed from the waist down and jumped into the swim trunks as if someone might walk in on me, tossing my socks and underwear into a nearby locker. On the way out, I realized my shirt was still on, and left it behind as well before returning to poolside. Pramin swam along the edge toward the far side, but stopped to egg me on. Jump

"Jump in!" he called.

I dipped one foot and found the temperature descent enough to jump right in. Water scurried away from my body on impact, but quickly settled back to a general stillness around me.

"I'm gonna finish this lap!" yelled Pramin, just before

I dove under, allowing my sweaty face and head to enjoy the cooling water. I pulled myself forward, one stroke at a time, through the thick body and opened my eyes to its bright blue beauty. But this didn't last long before tightness around my neck forced me to surface as Pramin entered the final stretch. My arms and legs fluttered to keep me afloat as I watched him draw closer, crashing through the water. But he dove under, and a moment of peace ensued. I could see light from above dance prettily against the water until he launched up in front of me to disrupt it.

"Wanna race?" he gasped.

"Nah, I'm good," I insisted.

"Or see who can stay under longer?"

I shook my head and Pramin stared off as if trying to think of what to say next. "Well what do you wanna do?"

"Honestly, I just want to relax for a bit," I said with a fake laugh.

"I know you're scared," Pramin sighed.

"Scared!?"

"Yeah, of TEO. I get it; I was- I still *am*."

Why is that? I wondered. Knowing what they were capable of was more than enough to strike fear into one's heart, but he spoke as if he'd had a history of his own with them.

"Wait, so you used to work for them too?"

"We all did, but Durai got us out before it was too late."

"So they went after you?" I asked.

"No, but he showed us the list with our names on it."

"What kind of list?"

"A list of people they didn't need anymore," he said. "And he told us about the crazy stuff they do, and what they've got planned."

This was the most out of the loop I'd ever felt, and the blame fell completely on my father. All of the one-on-one time with Bari after I stopped going to work with them had to be the backdrop for everything I'd missed out on. So the true capper was the day I saw something I wish I hadn't, thus beginning my hiatus.

"You good?" asked Pramin.

"Hm? Yeah," I said, emerging from deep thought. "I think I'm gonna go."

"What is it?"

"What's what?"

His eyes narrowed. "You know something, right? What is it?"

It's that obvious? I thought to myself. "I mean, it doesn't really matter. Can't help us anyway."

"Oh," he shrugged.

As nonchalantly as I acted, deep down, the opposite reaction was desired, as I knew it would help *me* to get this off my chest. "I saw him with her," I blurt out.

"Saw who?"

"My dad with some lady. Cause he used to take us to work with him, but he always made us wait in his office once he was done for the day. Never told us why though." Pramin already understood where this was going, but I continued nonetheless. "So one time when I heard him talking to somebody right out-side the door, I looked out." I awaited assurance that

117

Pramin still followed before proceeding. "And I saw my dad and her kissing. Only reason he pushed her off was cause he saw me watching," I said.

"What did he do then?" Pramin looked on.

"He started yelling at me like *I* did something wrong and I guess I believed it. Never even went back there again."

Pramin took a long pause, having no clue what to say. "You tell anybody?" he finally asked.

I shook my head. "Just you." As a teenager, it became clear to me that my father not only cheated on my mom, but he'd forced me, his own naive preschooler, into silence. No heartfelt apology-not even the release I now felt-was going to change that. But wallowing was pointless. "I think I'm gonna go back upstairs. "You good though? asked Pramin."

"Yeah, thanks, really."

"Well I'm here if you need me," he replied. "Oh, and the locker room has showers too."

I hopped onto the ledge, butt-first, spun on my tailbone and got up. "Thanks," I said, this time flashing a sincere smile which faded at the locker rooms entrance. I popped open the locker, housing my things and brought them with me straight ahead to the showers. My foot hit the small hump in the doorway, but I caught myself mid-fall, grasping the frame.

The ice-cold floor tiles bit into my feet as I grabbed a towel from a nearby rack and rushed in one of six shower pods, closing the curtain behind myself. Inside was a rectangular compartment, safe from the water, which I stuffed my trunks along with everything else into before cranking the knob to the hottest possible setting. I didn't even like hot showers-I hated them, and found lukewarm water much more preferable to bathe in. But my previous experience with showers taught me that they always start off colder than expected, and this time was no different. Water sprayed through the shower head at exactly the right temperature, but as it teetered toward the actual setting, I cranked it down to my sweet spot. With that in order, I turned to the soap dispenser and held my hand beneath it until at least six pumps of slick gel plopped down. As I distributed it throughout my body, it had a sting to it as if actively killing off both germs and pool chemicals alike. This feeling intensified while the soap was blasted away, turning its white pigment green before the drain snatched it down. Keeping my face and scalp out of dodge were major concerns as I repeated this process two more times.

Although I now felt clean, the shower was too comfortable to leave just yet; and what was the point of rushing back, anyway? All that awaited was the very same stress I needed this time away from. Plus, the others still had work to do on their gadgets, so it made sense for me to stay put. However, I quickly realized that standing idle in the shower left little more to do than think, and the unyielding thought, barreling back and forth across my mind was, of course, TEO. Who was I kidding?

I turned off the water and grabbed my incredibly fluffy towel from the packed compartment, being careful not to knock anything down. Once I dried off, and got dressed, I returned to poolside.

"Going back up?" asked Pramin, floating on his back.

"Yeah."

"Alright, you can drop your wet stuff in there," he pointed.

I turned my attention to a mailbox-like slot by the door, tossing my towel and trunks into it as I left.

"I'll be up in a minute!" called Pramin.

"Ok!"

I hurried back down the lonely hallway and called myself an elevator, sliding in before its doors could fully opened. This time, I bent down to see for myself what the panel said, and the options listed were the hotel lobby, lab, recreational center, and basement. I made the obvious choice which sent me back to the others who were now huddled around one table, looking over as I entered.

"What's up?" I asked, nervously walking over.

"Let him hear it," Durai told Rian who then passed me his rectangular touch-screen device. It had a video ready to be rewinded and when I did so, a New York reporter popped up, providing "breaking news". "A statewide search for Ivanna and Isaiah Abiah who are prime suspects in the deadly shooting of an African American religious leader earlier this afternoon is now underway." The screen panned out to make room for a picture. "In this surveillance video, you can see the two suspects, trying to blend into the crowd before hacking a nearby Enforcer to shoot the man and flee the scene. Anyone who sees suspicious activity is asked to contact local police immediately. The police force thanks you in advance for your cooperation."

The video ended and the room grew silent.

"This changes everything," said Durai.

"What do you mean?" I asked.

"You need to go surrender. I mean, they're clearly giving you the chance. They could've framed you and Jabari too but they didn't. Plus they didn't even put out pictures of these two, so they're still giving you a chance to do this the easy way. They'll find you regardless, so why not give yourselves up while you still can and be on their good side?"

He was right. This was a chance to at least tame this nightmare until an opportunity to end it arose.

"And working for them is temporary. I might not have been able to do it, but with somebody else on the inside, we can stop them; It'll take some time, is all."

"I'll go," I declared.

"Well, I'm going too," said Bari. "They want both of us."

"Yeah," said Ivanna.

"Look, you guys don't have to-"

"They're looking for us too," added Isaiah. "We're in this together now, Naaji."

"Then it's settled," proclaimed Durai. Could you take them down to the headquarters, Molly?

She nodded without a second thought and told us to come on. We followed her back to the elevator doors from whence we came, and they opened shortly after she pushed the button, allowing us to file in. From my position, backed against the center wall, I got a final glance at the others who'd gone right back to their work as the doors sealed. Silence overtook the elevator, and all of us stared straight ahead. Clearly, I wasn't the only one contemplating whether or not this was our best option- I couldn't be. We were about to walk right into the base of a secret society we knew next to nothing about except that no length-even murder- was too great in the pursuit of their desires. But the doors chimed back open, freeing us of our trance as people still buzzed around the lobby, albeit, mostly uniformed employees, while the five of us exited- this time, on our way to what very well could be our final stop.

CHAPTER 13: P.E

Four Striders were stationed at the front entrance of the towering skyscraper which managed to present the abbreviation of the establishments name even more proudly than Durai's hotel front.

"Hey! said Molly, gaining our attention. "Don't be stupid in there."

It wasn't exactly the greatest show of support but we took what we could get. Isaiah, Ivanna, Jabari and I were barely even out of the car before being apprehended by the Striders posted out front. Molly wasn't exempt from this either.

"Out of the vehicle, ma'am!" said one of the Striders.

"What? No, I'm just dropping them off!"

"Resistance will have consequences!" they said, raising their gatling guns.

"Alright, alright," she said, getting out of the car.

The Striders then brought us into the buildings lobby which had a good flow of people throughout, likely going to and coming from interviews. We were escorted to the elevators labeled "Staff only" which neighbored those designated for interviewees and were nudged into the abnormally large space once the doors opened. After entering a long passcode on the keypad above the handprint panel and buttons for the floors, the doors of the elevator resealed. Each Strider stood in its own corner looking at us in the middle.

"We're gonna be fine," whispered Molly. "I think."

The doors opened, and ahead of us was a straight red-carpeted path with at least ten black doors on either side, leading to one far larger than the others. The way was lit by a torch above every other door, and the walls were painted red.

"Move!" demanded one of them coldly.

Rather than grant myself time to consider all the ways things could go south, I speed walked down the hallway, closely followed by everyone else.

"Stop!" shouted a Strider as we neared the door. I followed its instruction and two of them proceeded by, knocking before opening the double doors together. On the other side of it were three wrinkly old bald men sitting next to each other on huge thrones within a large mostly empty room with black marble floors and red walls. The man to the far left had a thin pointy nose while the one to the right had thick nostrils, and slightly less drained skin than his counterparts. The middle man was identical to the one whom Durai had programmed the Mark 1 to look like. They all wore the same blood red hooded robes that Durai placed on the Accessible Strider. This was without a doubt the 1st Echelon.

"Hello, boys!" said the man in the middle.

"Glad you could join us," hissed the one to his left.

"Indeed," said the third.

"We thought you'd gotten cold feet once you changed addresses, but it looks like you just needed a bit of space to come to your senses," said the middle man.

"Space?" I asked. "You sent a Strider to kill us!"

"Wrong. We sent a Strider to *warn* you that there are consequences for disobedience," he said. "Now, it's time to make your decision. You can willingly work for us, and produce more of your inventions, or you we can make you our personal slaves right after we hang your friends in front of you."

Bari and I didn't say a word, though this wasn't a choice to begin with, and the others were frozen with fear.

"I think they're choosing the former," laughed the left-side man.

"Appears that way. So let's go through with the ritual."

"What are you talking about?" I asked nervously.

"It's a surprise!" said the obvious ringleader, smiling from ear to ear. These guys were just as crazy as advertised, and we were in over our heads. "Take the Busara brothers to the ritual prep room, Striders 1 and 2!" he shouted. "Striders 3 and 4, put the rest of them in cells."

"Yes, sir!" they said all at once.

They separated Ivanna, Isaiah, and Molly into the first three rooms on the halls right side, locking the sliding doors with passcodes on each of their panels. Bari and I, however, were brought to a door about halfway down the halls left side which opened automatically once we reached close proximity. No one was in the glaringly lit all white room containing long tables separated in two lines of three, all with syringes connected by tubes to empty blood packs atop them.

"Sit down!" barked the Striders. This obviously wasn't time for any bravery. Anything remotely close to resistance could bring us to a very violent end, so Bari and I sat together on red-cushioned bar stools at the nearest table to the right. Unconsciously, I rocked my foot up and down while my brain refused to produce anything aside from terrible thoughts.

"We're good," Bari assured. "Just do what they say."

But they didn't say anything. The Striders simply picked up two needles among many resting on metal trays and glared straight through us with blue yet somehow lifeless eyes as they turned our wrists over. It wasn't until they moved the razor sharp tips toward our veins, that I realized for the first time just how frightening my father's raw creation truly was. These weren't typical Striders doctored up to look exactly like real people, but rather naked and hollow silhouettes.

I groaned as the needle easily pierced my wrist and vein, sparking discomfort while Bari didn't even flinch Our blood rushing into the transparent syringes until the space was filled. The Striders reached between us for bandages, and separated them from the adhesives. They were quick to apply them on the area of incision immediately after extracting the needles. Our blood then rushed from the syringes, through tubes and into the awaiting packs which dangled nearby.

"Let's go!" ordered the Strider assigned to me. It's metallic voice bounced around the room. They unlatched the packs of our blood from the tubes as Bari and I rose, avoiding any abrupt movement. We were then prompted to proceed ahead of them and complied. *What do they need our blood for?* I wondered. The door breezed open for us to step back into the ominously silent hall we started in. My stomach contorted itself more and more with each step closer to the double doors housing the 1st Echelon.

Bari noticed my squirms. "Be cool," he whispered. I stopped short to gather myself, but received a rough nudge in the back. "Keep moving!" said the Strider. This was a pretty pointless command seeing as, a few steps later, we were told to stop so they could knock on and open up the double doors in dramatic fashion, revealing us to our captors once again.

"Back so soon?!" called the middle man from his throne.

Neither of us replied.

"Let the ritual commence!"

The other two Striders from before stood on either end of the trio who looked down at us.

"Well, don't be shy! We usually don't bite!" he said, motioning us closer to the marble stairs leading up to them. He stopped us at the bottom step before calling Striders 1 and 2 which then, very cautiously, walked upstairs in unison- their metal bottoms clinking gently as they went. It wasn't until they reached them that I noticed the men now each had a chalice studded with diamonds, which still managed to frolick in spite of faint lighting, resting on the arms of their thrones. I leaned toward Bari who was to my right to see what the Striders were doing with our blood packs, but felt instant regret. They'd punched holes in them and were distributing the blood into the chalices until none remained.

"Give these to our new employees," the middle man told each Strider, handing them very stiff-looking sheets of paper from his lap. They gingerly returned down the stairs to us and revealed our contracts, almost slashing through the flesh of my palm with its corner during the handoff of mine. There wasn't much of anything to the contracts though. One sentence that told us to sign below should we wish to pledge our minds, spirits, and bodies for the greater good of both the society and planet Earth was all it had to offer. No further explanation or even fine print, that I could see, made them, more or less, a waste of paper if you asked me.

"Write your initials on the line."

"You didn't even give us pens," I replied to the middle man.

"Just use the corner of the contracts to draw some blood," he said with a demented smile. "That will suffice."

I figured the interaction couldn't possibly get any more peculiar from here, however this sentiment jumped ship the instant we pricked our fingers on the contracts. The men put the chalices to their lips but paused, as if waiting for us to stain our sheets with bloody initials. Once we did the deed, they tipped them inward and were consuming the blood right before our eyes-Bari's eyes rather. I turned away the moment they began. *The hell is wrong with these guys?* I wondered to myself, while trying to recover from the chills which trickled down my back.

"That wasn't so hard, was it?" called the middle man from upstairs only to receive no answer from either of us in return.

"They don't talk much," the man left of him interjected, using a sleeve to drag leftover blood from his chin.

"So long as they're productive, that won't be an issue," the third man.

"Indeed," nodded the middle man. "Welcome to the society, boys!"

CHAPTER 14: NEWBIES

B ari and I began unpacking our creations along with all manner of tools needed for work on them. We'd been granted the opportunity by the 1st Echelon to retrieve our things and come right back to work. I found it odd that they allowed without sending escorts with us, but, then again, what would we really do? Run? Hide? For what, so they could hunt and drag us right back? They knew and we knew it was a pointless game of cat and mouse with the same exact conclusion time and time again. Our brief visit back to the lab with the others was just as dejected as our previous exit. The room we now inhabited shared the all-white interior of the one we got blood taken in. It had its differences though: There was a thick black line on the floor, splitting the room in half with the addition of only two tables, placed on either side, and, best of all, another human being. Live. In the flesh. Not another lifeless Strider mindlessly following orders while evoking little to no emotion in the process. My enthusiasm for us being placed alongside another person, however, was instantaneously smashed once I saw the stranger's eyes roll at us.

"Sorry," said the man, knowing he'd been caught. "It's not you, it's just, they told me I'd have a break from breaking newbies in, but I guess not." Bari still went about his business, fishing things out of our bag as if never hearing the man.

"It's cool," I told him. "What's your name anyway?"

He walked over to us and replied, "Paul," slicking down his greasy combover with one hand while reaching to shake mine with the other. His beard neatly stretched out from his face and was just as blond as that on his head. He damn near crushed my hand with his deathgrip.

"Naaji," I said.

Bari finally spoke up. "Jabari," he told Paul. They shook hands.

"Pleasure to meet ya," smiled Paul. "You two new here, or just changed floors?"

"It's our first day."

Paul's eyes focused in on the table where our ESGs and EDPs awaited attention from us. "You mind?" he asked halfway reaching at them. I gestured for him to proceed. "What are they?" He now held one of each creation in each hand.

"That's an Electromagnetic Stasis Grenade," Bari cut in, pointing to his left hand. "And that's an Electric Discharge Pistol," he added, now aimed at his right.

I tip-toed for a look at his table. "Where's your invention?"

"Oh, I'm not an inventor; I'm one of the supervisors."

He tucked his button-down further into his pants.

So you're one of them, huh? I thought to myself. But maybe he wasn't. I mean, he didn't act like it. He didn't talk or look like the maniacs we'd just encountered before meeting him. This guy was easily the first normal person to interact with us since stepping foot in the building, and having an ally on the inside was an asset I refused to let slip away. "So, how long you been working here?"

"Its my second year."

"And you're supervising already?" asked Bari, eyebrows raised.

"Yup. A lot of people come and go around here, so there's plenty room to move up."

I gulped at the potential implications of this statement. "So what do we do while we're here, just tweak our inventions?"

"Sure. And of course you gotta come up with fresh new ideas as you go. Longevity is everything," he said, tightening up his face to place even more gravity upon his words. "But anyway, for today I'll just be giving you guys a quick tour and run-down of everything." He brought us to the exit which promptly slid out of the way. The hallway on this floor was far more hotel-like than its spacious counterpart, housing the 1st Echelon members in charge of this headquarters. Paul walked ahead of us toward the dead end, opposite to the elevator down the other end of the corridor, but turned his head to speak to us. "Ok, so like I said, the main responsibilities you two have are making sure you're productive at all times. When you're not perfecting an invention, you better be working out ideas for new ones, and when you aren't doing that, you better be collaborating with someone else in your department to get something of theirs done. That's the job description. "You get me?"

Bari and I both nodded. "Good," he said. We now stood directly in front of a large words-one on top of the other-which read, *New Additions.* Paul hovered one palm beneath the bold lettering. "If you haven't guessed it already, this floor is designated for new-comers." If not for my terrible eyesight, I would have seen it the moment the elevator doors opened, as intended.

"Cool," I said, masking a cough.

"There aren't a whole lot of rooms on this floor in use, but I'll introduce you to some people you'll probably be collaborating with while you're here." We made way for Paul to step between us and lead. I counted at least ten doors lining either side of the hall as we walked down it. Paul stopped dead in his tracks and knocked on the door to his immediate left. I couldn't understand the logic behind this since he placed a hand on the scanner panel beside the door, opening it without ever hearing a peep from the other side. "What's up, guys?" he asked whomever was in the room. "We've got some more-" Paul searched left and right for us before spinning around to see Bari and I still staring in from the doorway. "Don't be shy. C'mon in." I slapped Bari's arm for him to enter and followed close behind as he did. "This is Naaji and Jabari," Paul told the two men. Their baby faces, devoid of any facial hair whatsoever told me they were our age or younger. "This is Keith and Keon," he said after momentarily squinting at their nametags.

We moved in closer to shake their hands. Bari shook Keon's while I shook Keith's and we swapped afterwards, briefly exchanging cordial words amongst ourselves. There was something off about them though. They were both awkwardly positioned, blocking our view of whatever was on their tables, but I wasn't about to call them out on it.

"Well ugh, I guess you'll all see each other later on. We've got a few more things to handle," smiled Paul before leading the way back to the door.

"See you later, Paul," replied Keith.

Bari beat me to the punch, asking Paul exactly what I'd planned to once the door closed behind us. "What's their deal?"

"Huh?" replied Paul.

"They acted like they didn't want us to see their stuff."

"Oh yeah. Cause they didn't."

"Why not?" I budded in.

Paul gently face-palmed. "I almost forgot to tell you my number 1 tip for newbies: It's always a good idea to be super careful about who you let see your inventions. You don't want anyone stealing your ideas, so I suggest you take my advice." On the opposite side of the hall, a few doors down, we entered another room and swiftly repeated the introduction process. This pair of inventors weren't any more keen on allowing us to see what they were working on than the first had been. "Alright," said, Paul, "now we can go to the Worker Aid floor."

"What for?" asked Bari.

"Just a few formalities; nothing crazy.

Speaking of crazy, why the hell did the 1st Echelon drink our blood, anyway? I knew this wasn't the most appropriate way to go about asking my question, so I kept this format in my head where it belonged, instead using a more conservative one. "So what's up with that ritual thing they made us do?" I asked as politely as I could.

"Couldn't tell you if I tried. If it makes you feel any better, they do that with everybody they give contracts to, so it's nothing personal." Paul looked ahead as we approached the elevator, but I almost wanted him to turn and see my reaction. Did he actually think that's what we'd want to hear? Of all the things he could have gone with, he chose that? I just barely heard the elevator call button click as Paul pressed it. Once it arrived and we boarded, rather than enter a long code on the keypad like the Strider had when initially escorting us to the 1st Echelon, Paul simply placed his hand on the scanner pad and chose one of the floor numbers which lined the wall. The instant the doors reopened, every grain of silence was smothered by all manner of sound, from indistinct chatter between voices, to phone chimes, to the oh-so satisfying clicks and clacks of keyboards. Even though these were commonplace conditions within office cubicles, I found this one odd. Something was far different about this noise: it was even more powerful. But I could see the amount of room wasn't larger than any other set of cubicles would have been, so that wasn't the issue.

"Naaji?" called Paul, snapping me from my daze to see he and Bari standing on the outside awaiting my exit. "Yeah," I replied.

He used his foot to block the door from automatically closing. "You coming?" I awkwardly exited without saying anything back. "Everything alright?"

"Uh, yeah, I was just thinking," I assured before he spun around to take us to our next destination.

"What are we doing on this floor again?" asked Bari.

"You don't like surprises do you?" teased Paul.

"Not really, no."

"Right now, you two are getting your IDs." As we turned the corner to walk up the outer left of the cubicles, I began to catch glimpses of men and women dressed in formal attire, typical of an office, actually working up a sweat.

"Was that just a Strider in that cubicle with them?" asked Bari. I had no clue which one he'd seen where this was the case or how I missed it. *Oh yeah, I'm pretty much legally blind,* I remembered.

"Sure was," replied Paul. "When somebody's not doing their job effectively enough, they need a little push."

"Oh, ok," I jumped in. I refused to allow him to say anything more on the subject. Paul had a bad habit of saying exactly what one *wouldn't* want to hear. "So how far's the room?"

"Not far at all. Why? Tired already?"

"No I-"

"Oh, yeah, like I was saying, when a supervisor sees a workers isn't working hard enough, they can call a Strider to bring the best out of them."

That's not all they're bringing out, I thought after seeing one sweating straight through his dress shirt. "What's everybody doing?"

"The usually corporate dirty work: taking business calls, setting inventors up with appointments, managing the organizations money, blah blah blah. That kind of stuff." He stopped and slightly cracked open the wooden door to his left. "Can we come in?" he asked, peeking in.

"Of course!" called a voice from within. We all entered the room which was filled to the brim with a lemon fragrance as well as light from the camera set up, complete with backdrop and reflective posts. The woman whom we joined in the room appeared to be in her mid-late 40's, but I certainly wasn't going to ask her for confirmation. "New additions, Paul?" she asked, shooing hair out of her face with extended pink-polished nails.

"Yes, ma'am," he replied.

The woman proceeded to ask our names and we told her. "Alright, step in front of the backdrop for me, dear," she told me. I obliged and found myself blitzed by the full force of the lighting. She came over and adjusted my body and head until I was perfectly centered across from the camera at the peak of a tripod. "Smile," said the unknown woman while doing just that herself. I gave her the most unintentionally awkward smile in recent memory. You would think, with the already blinding lights facing the backdrop, there was no need for flash on the camera itself. However, I indeed *was* made subject to it. The abrupt output of light momentarily burned a circular figure into my retina. "You're all done," said the camera lady. She called Bari over for his turn and gave him the same treatment she did me. The computer monitor sitting on a nearby desk now displayed my picture, though I saved myself the embarrassment of taking anything more than a glance at it. I always hated hearing myself talk, and seeing myself in videos or awkward pictures like the one I'd just taken. The woman walked over by the computer desk where the space was also shared with a fancy looking printer. A few mouse clicks later and an blunt-edged rectangular card shot halfway out of the perfectly sized printer slot. I again ignored the actually photo when she handed it to me, instead using my thumb to appreciate the ID cards glossiness. I was just about to slide it into my pocket when she said, "Hold on," reaching into a drawer and pulling out a black lanyard with the organizations name fully written out in white letters along each strip. I snapped the metal clip at the end of it onto my ID and stuck my head through the loop.

Bari displayed none of my awkwardness when getting his picture taken. When the camera clicked, he flashed his pearly whites right back at it. The monitor now displayed his head shot rather than mine, and the lady printed out Bari's ID card, handing it off to him alongside a lanyard.

"You're all set, boys."

"Thanks, Audrey," said Paul, backing his way to the door. He then motioned us to do the same and we did.

"No trouble at all," smiled Audrey. "See you around."

The three of us left the room in order of Paul, Bari, then me back to the noisy cubicles. "Almost done," Paul assured. But his tone indicated the opposite instead of agreeing with this statement.

"What else is there?" I asked.

"You're gonna need your handprints in the system."

"What, for the elevators?"

"Yeah, and certain doors."

"So we can to any floor we want?.."

"For you and Naaji, it'll only be good for this floor and New Additions until you get promoted," Paul told him.

"How long does that take?"

"Depends on your production speed."

"So-"

"When an inventor from any department thinks they have a finished product, they can request an examination by the 1st Echelon. And if it's accepted, you get an assigned time to bring whatever your invention is to the Throne Room for a demonstration." Paul caught his breath.

"And then what?" I asked, unintentionally impatient.

"If they're impressed, you get a nice raise to your paycheck and they start mass producing your invention," he continued. "But in you guy's case, whenever you go for examination, they'll assign you to a department on a new floor so you can tweak your inventions.

Then, you'll be able to get those other perks after your follow-up examination if it goes well."

"And what if it doesn't?" Bari took the words right out of my mouth.

"If they feel like the invention's good but needs work, they'll send you back to work more on it for awhile before you can get another examination." He paused. "And if they think it's not useful at all, you get let go."

"Our stuffs ready to go," I replied in confidence. "So can we just get our examination out of the way now?"

Paul gestured in a halting manner. "Well, lets not get ahead of ourselves. I mean, it *is* only your first day. You're better off just getting the easy stuff done today. Trust me." As much as I wanted to argue against this- and I'm sure Bari did too- neither of us said a word in contention. Paul was the one with experience here, and had a genuine vibe about him. It was clear he really wanted others, especially those under his wing, to do well. We walked further down the cubicles left side perimeter until reaching a set of three ATM like machines. Two were occupied, leaving the far-side one for us.

"This is a self-service station," said Paul, pointing at the machine. "You can come here whenever you need certain things done on your own." He turned to face the screen. "Gimme a sec." I took a moment to just look around, but there wasn't much character on the floor. Bland gray filled the spaces walls, ceiling, cubicles, and floor. They tried to liven things up with obviously artificial tall-standing plants posted near every other cubicle entrance. Whoever's idea this was must not have realized it only served to further torture the eyes of anyone forced to look at the setup for hours at a time. One of the two others walked away.

Paul told me to step up. "Put your hand on the screen." Upon doing this, I saw a prompt asking that I keep my hand there while my prints were scanned.

"Handprint scanned!" said a soft voice through the speakers on either side of the machine. A few button pushes later, Paul called Bari to step up for his turn. Before I knew it, he was done too.

"Alright, you're good to go," said Paul. "Now you can get your checks."

"Checks?" I asked.

"Or cash if you want."

"Yeah, but I mean we're getting paid already?"

"You unless you like working for free," said Paul.

"I mean, I just expected it at the end of the week I guess."

"Nope. We get paid daily."

Paid daily? How rich are these people?

"Next place we're going's the front desk." We returned to the elevator with a bit more urgency, knowing our run-around was almost over. Paul greeted the other person already occupying it and hit the lobby button after scanning his hand. "Oh yeah you guys can get to the lobby by yourselves too." The doors reopened and the three of us made way for the other person, receiving a mumbled, "thank you," in return. The elevator continued on its way, picking up and letting off others until finally reaching the lobby. There were five lines of people waiting to be helped by workers at the front desk.

Paul wasn't having it. "Screw that," he said. "C'mon." He walked us to the nearest edge of the counter. "'cuse me," he called for someones attention. A woman in uniform turned toward us. "Can you help us out real quick, Sheena?" She asked the man across from her for a moment before walking over to us. Her red-dyed dreads hung down, some in front of her, some behind. "What's up, Paul?"

"They need their checks," he told her, pointing to us.

"Names?"

"Naaji and Jabari," he paused. "What's your last name?" Paul asked us.

"Busara," I told Sheena.

"Got it." She walked back over to her station and opened a drawer behind the desk and pulled out two small sheets of paper. She briefly scribbled on each of them before speed walking back over to us. "I spelled your names right?"

I stared down to scan the checks when she handed them over. "Yeah, thanks."

"Mhm," Sheena smiled before returning to her post. I realized I'd neglected to even look at how much we were being paid and immediately glanced down at my check. Twenty-five thousand dollars was made out to me, and before I could even peek over at Bari's, Paul was right back on us.

"We got one more stop," he said as he walked away

"Where?" I asked.

But instead of answering, he motioned us to follow

him into the half closed elevator doors. I did my best not to intrude the space of fellow riders which became tiresome as the car stopped on damn-near every floor for newcomers and departures. It certainly didn't help that Paul waited for everyone else to clear out before setting course where we needed to go next. "I'm just showing you guys the museum," he finally answered.

However, when the doors opened for us to step out, I was admittedly disappointed. There were no artifacts; no never-before-seen technology from any golden age. Not even a glorifying portrait in sight. There was only the eeriness of our dancing shadows sprung from the obviously artificial torches, lining the right hand wall. Opposite to the elevator, however, was an altar and upon it, an open book, thick with pages made readable by two more fake torches on either side.

I squinted at the set of words on top. "What's it say?"

"Les éclairés," said Paul. "The Enlightened Ones. A Frenchman started the society when he was thirty-two/three."

"What year?" Bari asked.

"1831."

"So the society's been around all this time and hasn't been found out? How's that even possible?"

"It's always had great cover ups like TEO, plus anyone who *could* be a threat gets taken care of."

"Well know even is the guy that started all this? What's his name?"

"No clue. All we know him as is the Grandmaster, and

no one outside the 1st Echelon gets to see him. Shit, *they* barely even see him."

"Well who wants to see a grave anyway?" I shrugged.

"Oh yeah," Paul cheesed, "he's not dead."

I didn't need math to be unsettled by this. "You just said he was thirty-something in eighteen-whatever."

"If I knew, I'd tell you," he sighed. "But it's not our concern either way. Just do your job."

"That's what we're trying to do," Bari protested.

"Good. This book's here to help you with that; it's got all of the society's philosophies."

"So we're supposed to stand here and read the whole thing?" I asked.

"Of course not. Just understand who we are and why we're here." Knowing our ignorance, he continued. "When the Grandmaster started the society, he did it with the mindset that anyone smart or powerful enough to bend the world to their will had every right to do so. Anyone unworthy of this would serve the cause one way or another. And that's the gist of it."

"But how did he even start all this by himself back then?" asked Bari.

"The wealthy and powerful want to stay that way forever, and it wasn't hard at all back then to get in touch with them. So when the Grandmaster gave them his pitch, of course they got in on it and funded him," said Paul. "Anything else?"

All I could think about was clocking out of that Hell hole for the day, and Bari certainly shared the same sentiment. Neither of us said a word, and we were then brought back to the lobby.

"Now you're done for today, guys," said Paul. I couldn't believe how smoothly this all was going. But, then again, it's difficult to go anywhere but up after having watched old men, or anyone for that matter, gulp down your blood.

"So what time do we come in for work tomorrow?" asked Bari.

"You'll be here already."

"What do you mean?" I asked.

"Sorry guys, but they need you to work a little overtime for now," said Paul, lowering his voice to a whisper. His eyebrows flared upward as he said this, telegraphing exactly what he really meant: *You two aren't leaving until they say so.*

"Well what're we supposed to do?"

"Work, I guess," Paul shrugged.

"But you just said we were done for today," Bari protested.

"You can go to your chambers then," said Paul, frustrated. "What can I say? You guys screwed around and pissed them off. This is what happens. Just remember what I said, and don't dig yourselves deeper." Paul walked away, leaving the two of us standing there speechless. "Hope to see you around," he mumbled.

I wondered to myself if Paul had super-human abilities, and legitimately leaned toward believing he did. He must have somehow mastered telepathy, I just knew it. How else could he have known to withhold such a crucial aspect of our current standing until the very moment I began seeing some upside in all this.

"What now?" asked Bari.

My mind began to race as I weighed our options, and all but one were unfavorable. "Get on their good side." Bari gave me a look of confusion. "We gotta do the examination. I'm pretty sure it'll help if we show them we're useful," I explained. "That's what Paul kept saying."

"Yeah, you're right. Let's try to get an appointment ASAP."

"Where do we-" Bari pointed past and turned me by the shoulder to see another set of self-service machines by the elevators which we hurried over to. The home screen of the one we chose displayed many options, including examination requests and scheduling. When pushed, this opened another page where we had to enter our names and request examination for any given date and time.

"Tomorrow morning?" asked Bari.

"I guess."

"Ight," he replied, punching in the appointment we wanted. After sending the request, a notification soon popped up to tell us it had been received by the 1st Echelon. This was followed by another one before we could even return to the main menu. It said our request for examination had been accepted. "That was quick."

A little too quick, I thought. Were they expecting us so soon or did they just sit around waiting for appointments to be made? That couldn't be; they had far more to concern themselves than such trivial matters. Secretary's were my best guess. But I quickly reverted back to the task at hand.

"Let's see what our room's like," I said, calling an elevator.

"You tired too?" asked Bari. He actually seemed relieved.

"Not really, but what else can we do?"

"True."

When the doors parted, we made way for the elderly couple who came waddling out, and they thanked us in unison.

"You're welcome," I mumbled.

But Bari stopped me halfway into the shaft. "Wrong one," he said.

"Huh?" I frowned.

"Don't we take the worker ones?"

He was absolutely right. "Oh yeah, my bad." I played off the mistake and quickly moved to the employee side before anyone else saw. When *these* doors opened, no one was on the other side. My palm was warmed by the panel as it scanned before revealing our floor among other options. It was a straight shot up there once I set the destination.

Bari stepped out first. "Which one was it again?" he asked.

"Over here," I said, taking the lead. At our door, he jumped in front of me to try unlocking it with his own print. Yet another plain white space greeted us when it opened, this time with the additions of a bunk-bed and TV up on the wall. But it was far smaller than our work area- about the size of an average jail cell.

"Hello!" said a robotic voice, startling us once the doors closed. "Welcome to your quarters. My name is Gerri, and I'm the building's designated worker A.I. Just call my name and I'll answer any questions or concerns you have. You can turn me off at any time by saying, 'Gerri, power off.' Is this all understood?"

"Yes."

There was a pause before the voice said, "Ok," and went silent. I plopped down on the bottom bed, adjacent to the desk and chair while Bari walked to the door.

I sat up and asked where he was going.

"Bathroom," he replied. But the door wouldn't budge even as he waved his hands to trigger a sensor.

"Gerri," I called.

"What can I help you with?"

"Open the door."

"I'm sorry, but I can't do that. Once you enter your quarters, you have essentially clocked out for the day and have to stay there until 4AM the following day. Do you understand?"

Bari looked like he was going to be sick, but held himself together. He kicked off both shoes and climbed up to the top bed. I was too proud of his surprising composure to even ask if he was alright.

"Gerri," I said.

"What can I help you with?"

"Turn on the TV."

"Sure!" The television, hanging above the doorway switched on, showing a game of baseball, and a remote control lit up on the desk. "The remote is here if you'd like to change the channel."

I grabbed and offered it to Bari as he stared up at the ceiling. "You can put something on," he said. But I could care less what was on the screen, so long as it provided decent background noise. When I sat the remote back in its place, I noticed a see-through container nearby and took a closer look, spinning it around in search of any label.

"Gerri."

"What can I help you with?"

"What're these pills on the desk?"

"The pills in the clear bottle are psychological enhancement supplements. All worker quarters have them."

"What kind of enhancements do they give?"

"They grant the user a boost in thought process and productivity," said Gerri. "But it is recommended that you only take one every five hours."

I turned to see what Bari thought, but he'd already drifted off to sleep. His exhaustion was warranted, so I left him be and scanned the bottled. I found it's supposed effects potentially useful. Who knew what the two of us- no- every inventor in the building was capable of with such enhancements. We'd all been able to create great things individually without them, after all. If a good chunk of us came together, plus Durai and the others, the 1st Echelon wouldn't stand a chance. But before any of that, I had to gauge the power of these pills for myself. Their container popped right open with a squeeze and twist of the cap so I could crane one out. It was chalky in my mouth as I struggled to gulp it down, cringing with each attempt until finally succeeding.

"Gerri."

"What can I help you with?"

"How long does it take for the pills to start working?" I asked.

"The effects of the psychological enhancement pills should set in immediately after taking one."

But I felt no difference. There weren't tons of new ideas flowing and I wasn't smarter than ever.

"Gerri, the pills didn't do anything."

"Not likely. The psychological enhancement pills have a ninety-five percent success rate."

Well I'm the other five percent, I thought. Risking an overdose to try another wasn't very appealing either, so that was that; my idea immediately made bust. However, I knew I could still find comfort elsewhere, and sat on the floor, crossing my legs. I breathed softly, focusing on each contraction and the movements that came with them until it felt like I was sinking. As always, I tried to find a place of balance but this time to no avail.

I just kept sinking. But it wasn't the bad or out of control kind. Had that been the case, I would've quickly opened my eyes to escape. It actually felt like an easy descent that eventually came to a hovering halt on its own. The darkness behind my eyelids suddenly grew warmer and warmer as a figure seemed to materialize in front of me. It was a man-like figure: a literal silhouette with no distinctive features beyond that.

"Hello," said the mystery figure.

Maybe they did work, I thought to myself.

"What, the pills? Yes, they *did* work." he replied.

"How'd you hear me?" I asked aloud.

"I'm your inner consciousness, nothing you say or think gets by me."

This wasn't my first encounter with this entity, but it *was* our first verbal exchange. Previously, he'd tried gesturing to communicate, but I couldn't make anything out. Even Isaiah said he had the same issue in his own experience.

So that's what you've been trying to tell me all this time? I asked.

"Actually, there is much more to learn," he said. "By communicating with me, your inner consciousness, you can tap into the space of your mind."

What can I do with that?

"To unlock the space of ones mind is to fully understand oneself. To master it is to transcend mortal capabilities."

How do you mean?

"You can take a form like my own and travel through the space of both your own mind and others."

But there wasn't much to explore from the looks of it. Before I could even address it, my conscience said,

"There is much more to this place. I will show you." The small area around him suddenly expanded before me, revealing a much larger version of our home in the now brightened background. I tried to approach it, forgetting I wasn't on that level yet.

When can I move around in here?

"In due time. Just like anything else, you will improve

with tireless ambition and practice over time. But for now, you must watch from a distance."

I was immediately thankful for this as a towering gold statue of my father sprung up dangerously close through the ground, standing on a pedestal between the house and I. It was blinding to gaze upon, and clearly my innermost self knew this as he swiftly banished it from my sight, leaving only the house.

What does all this mean? I asked.

"It is your inner domain. Everyone has one of their own, and what lies inside is a limitless space, filled by things, good and bad, that have affected your heart and soul throughout your lifetime."

Can you show me?

"The inner domain is sacred and you must enter for yourself." I assumed this was where the form like his own would come into play and he quickly confirmed this. "However, I must warn you, in your current state it is best not to overextend yourself by staying here much longer."

The house drifted off like dust in the air.

Wait no, I begged.

"You can return here some time in the future, but for now, your mind must rest."

My innermost self disappeared and I was quickly elevated back to the physical world, opening my eyes.

"Bari!" I said, springing up. "You sleep?"

"Almost was," he complained. "What's up?"

"You know that thing that's been trying to talk to me when I meditate?"

"What about it?"

"It like brought me into my own head and talked to me."

Bari's eyes widened. "What did it say?"

I easily fired off what was told to me, but felt my breaths get shorter with each detail until I collapsed. Everything was a blur but Bari, and soon others, tending to me as I slipped in and out of consciousness. Unidentifiable faces surrounded. Light fixtures streamed by. There was no pain, but I couldn't shake whatever ailment this was; not until I was stuck in the arm, that is. At this point, the woozy feeling began to simmer down and fazed out completely in about a minute's time. I'd been moved to a whited out room where two men, sporting lab coats stood to my left and right.

"What just happened to me?"

"We need you to relax," said one of them.

"Why'd you strap me down? I didn't do anything."

"You didn't do anything wrong, but you *did* have an allergic reaction to your enhancement pills. So we just need to run some tests."

"Well could you let me up, at least? And how long's all this gonna take?"

"Listen, we're just following procedure," he said. "And it'll take three to five days minimum."

"Five days?! I've got an appointment with the 1st Echelon tomorrow."

"Last name?" he asked, now at his monitor.

"Busara," I said quickly.

"Alright, we'll reschedule that for you."

"But-

"Look, we just need you to work with us."

"Why don't we let him get something to eat and then we'll run our tests?" asked his coworker.

It only took a moment for the first man to begrudgingly agree and let me loose. "*You* take him," he said.

Before entering the cafeteria a few doors down, I glanced at a set of doors leading out of this area. But they were locked without a doubt so making a move right then was pointless. I'd just have to wait things out until an opportunity presented itself.

"Hard choice?" asked the next man in line.

I checked his reflection through the vending machine before turning. "Oh, you can go, my bad."

"You're fine," he laughed. "The food in here's crap and the machine's free, so we always clean it out."

"Gotcha."

"I got a table over there if you wanna sit."

"Uh, sure, thanks," I replied, quickly making a selection before being led there past multiple other patients chomping their food down.

"So," he began, "the hell's a celebrity doing down here."

"What're you talking about?" I blushed.

"You're Naaji Busara. The whole world knows you."

"They know my dad."

"Eh, good point. But *I* know you. And your brother too," he said. "That's why I'm not understanding what you're doing in the detention center. They must not have realized who you are."

"Detention center? They said they're just running some tests."

"I'm guessing the pills didn't work on you."

"No, they *did*, I was like inside my own head and this thing was telling me all about how spirits in our minds work."

"They really laced the hell out of yours, huh," he mocked. "The most that ever happened to the rest of us was a bunch of vomiting."

"I kinda passed out," I said.

"Well, regardless, don't believe whatever crap they fed you about just 'running some tests'. You're here so they can make the pills strong enough to beat your immune system. They'll act like you're sick or your body's the problem but they just wanna figure out a better pill that'll have you hooked and easier to control. And-"

He stopped himself short, staring up behind me.

"We apologize for the inconvenience. You're welcome to go back to your post upstairs."

I was ecstatic about returning to our cell-like room, and all things considered, who could blame me? Certainly not this nameless soul across the table, who now shewed me off. I jumped up and followed the scientist
to freedom. Both my sudden removal and his change of body language told me they'd realized who I was, and wanted no part of disrupting our impending visit to see the 1st Echelon. He wouldn't even shoot a glance while sending me on my way back upstairs.

Bari hopped off his seat the instant I returned. "What'd they do to you?

"I'll tell you about it later, but I think I'm good. Let's

just get ready for tomorrow."

CHAPTER 15: SAVE OUR SOULS

The following morning, there wasn't a thing that my stomach would accept from the vending machines or food court. Uncertainty concerning our impending fate was eating me alive. If this didn't work out we could be in even worse standing with them. I was sure of this because of how Paul shoved the same point about being useful and productive down our throats. I knocked on the throne room door which had a Strider at either side and heard a loud yell from the other side, telling us to enter.

"You ready, bro?" asked Bari.

"No," I replied, pushing the door open.

The 1st Echelon got right to the point. "What do you have for us, boys?" said the middle man.

The stuff you would literally kill for, I thought. "Elec-"

"Oh the ESGs and EDPs, correct?" asked the left side guy.

"Yeah," Bari jumped in.

"Well, lets see them." We'd only brought one of each from our room and both shivered in my hands. Bari placed a crumbled up piece of paper on the floor a safe distance away and backpedaled to his former position at my side. I activated the ESG and gently rolled it near the paper. The men's faces lit up when the paper was caught up in the bubble it produced, but they didn't say anything. Bari went over, kneeling to close and grab the ESG, causing the paper to fall back down. Once he moved, I aimed at it with the EDP and pulled the trigger. However, I failed to realize the dial was cranked to the maximum output setting, so the paper, along with the marble floor surrounding it, was blown to pieces.

"Hey!" scolded the left man. Middle man put his hand out to calm him.

"It's fine, we'll fix it later," he said before looking down at us. "Well done, boys, you passed." *That was easy.* "You can move up to the-" he paused and the three of them murmured briefly. "Congratulations, you're promoted to the Gadgetry Department!" They all clapped as much as their tired hands would allow them to.

"What floor is that even on?" I asked.

"Use the handprint scanner in the elevator. The floors you're able to go to will light up." said the right man."

"We have to update it?" asked Bari.

"What do you mean?"

"Like how we added our handprint for the New Additions floor."

"We'll take care of that for you."

Remembering the reason we'd so hastily decided to have this examination in the first place, I said, "We can go home, right?" I was never very good at beating around the bush.

"Of course you can't," replied Middle Man, spitting on our hope. "You don't have that privilege after all it took to get you here."

Bari grabbed my arm. He could tell I was about to do something dumb by the fist one hand was balled into and our EDP tapping my leg in the other. "Chill, bro." He nodded at the 1st Echelon, thanked them for the promotion and pulled me with him to the exit.

"Good luck!" called one of them in a tone which annoyed me further.

Once we were a good distance from the doors and the Striders guarding them, I asked Bari why we didn't handle the 1st Echelon right then and there. We literally had a perfect shot at them.

"Dumb idea," he replied. I pressed him for an explanation and he pointed out that there was a shield in front of them.

"What are talking about?"

"They got a forcefield around them. It was there the first time we went in too. Didn't you see it?"

"Obviously not," I said, still hot.

"Aye, don't get mad at me 'cause you're eyes are trash." He wasn't wrong, but I didn't want to hear it. Besides, he knew full well I'd had more than my fill of people saying I need glasses.

"Shut up, bro," I told him, calling the elevator.

"I'm just saying. But whatever, what do we do now?"

"Just keep trying, I guess." I glanced over at the door of the room Bari and I slept in the evening prior.

Staying in that cramped space any longer than necessary was the last thing either of us wanted. Our elevator arrived and I placed a palm on the scanner upon entry until our options for floors lit up amongst the rows of others. Four were available: Lobby, Worker Aid, New Additions, and the Throne Room floor.

"Guess it didn't update yet," I said, pressing the button for New Additions. In an ideal world, our next course of action would have been to simply improve the ESGs and EDPs, but there weren't any viable additions that we hadn't already incorporated. Sitting on our hands and pretending to upgrade them would not go unnoticed, so that was a no-go. This left only one other option for us to appear useful. As I looked over at him, Bari's face was painted in contemplation until our stop was reached.

"We're gonna have to help some people out," I said once we disembarked.

"Yeah, inventors, right? I was thinking that. Who though?"

"We'll see when we get to whatever the new floor is." Speed walking down the hall, we reached our lab in what had to be record time. We had left our things in their usual bag underneath the table which I unzipped and gently placed our things from examination into.

"He left us a note," said Bari.

I looked up at him. "Huh?"

"Paul," he replied, handing me a sticky note. "He left

this."

Hey, I don't remember if I told you this, but always make sure you wear your IDs when you're in the building so Striders won't give you any trouble. Come by my office(room 103) on the Worker Aid floor if you need anything. - Paul

Yes, we *did* need something: a list of inventors in our department who needed extra help would have been nice. But this wasn't conveniently on the note nor would Paul have known off the top of his head whom such people were, and to assume otherwise was wishful thinking. I tucked the note into my pocket and swung the bag over a shoulder before we again left the room. The elevator took longer than usual both to arrive and reach our now available new floor. We could hear faint noises coming from rooms on either side of the hall as we made our way down it. A clear difference from New Additions was that each door here had at least one name lit up green on a rectangular screen above the scanner pads. Room after room we passed didn't have our names until Bari saw the one which did.

"Here we go," he said followed by unlocking it with his print. A voice welcomed us to the department through the speaker. This room didn't stray away from the generic all white format of our last. However, before even reaching either of the tables separated by the painted line, a loud whimper broke all silence, scaring us half to death. We looked around until locating its source: a man curled up in the corner left of the entryway.

"Sorry," he said, whipping tears from his face, "I was just leaving."

"Hold up, what happened?" asked Bari.

"They're kicking me out."

Wish they'd kick us out, I thought before realizing the gravity of his statement. "Wait so-"

"So I'm dead," he interrupted. "I wasn't good enough. I didn't do enough."

Bari gave him a look of sympathy. "What're you gonna do now?"

"I don't know," he sniffed.

A thought came to my mind. "We'll help you!" I blurted.

"How?"

"We know a guy that can sort it out for you; we just gotta go to his office."

"Paul?" asked Bari.

"Mhm." I helped the man up from his wallowing position, getting a close-up of the heavy bags beneath his eyes. From top to bottom, the man looked rough: his hair was a mess, lab coat in shambles, and face drenched in sweat.

"What's your name?" asked Bari while dusting him off.

"Oscar," he replied. "Oscar Judes."

"I'm Jabari, he's Naaji." We exchanged handshakes.

"Pleasures mine."

I dropped our stuff in the corner and put an arm over Oscar's shoulder, leading him out of the room. We needed someone to help and he was our guy, so I wanted to make the most of it. "Where you from?" I asked him on the way to the elevator.

"Boston," he proudly replied.

"And what's your invention?"

"I made these goggles to see through walls." This seemed like a pretty decent idea. "So why do they wanna get rid of you?"

"'Cause its already been done better."

Unsure what to say, I gave him a dry, "Oh."

"Yeah, so I don't know what else to do."

"We gotchu," Bari assured, clearly sharing my view of the big picture here.

We took the elevator to Worker Aid and made it through the chaos once again, this time, finding Paul's office. After a few knocks, he yelled for us to come in. "What's up?"

"This is Oscar Judes," I replied, holding my hands towards him, "and he needs some help."

"Ok?" said Paul rolling closer to his cluttered desk. I glanced at some photos of him with others over on the wall.

"Well, we just thought you might be able to help out."

"With what?"

"They wanna fire him, but-"

"Nothing I can do, sorry," he said, leaving us all speechless. "If they don't want him here, that's the end of it."

"But there's gotta be s-"

"The answer's no. Let it go."

Oscar looked ready to ball his eyes out at any moment

and Bari couldn't believe what he was hearing, leaving me to speak up. "But what about your note?"

"What about it? I said I'd help you guys out; I never said anything about somebody who's getting fired."

"So that's it?"

"Pretty much, yeah. Their decisions are final. Nothing personal," he said, looking at Oscar.

"Well, what if we help him get his stuff together?"

"I'm sure he's way past that if they want him gone." His face, for once, was incredibly stern. "Sorry, but if there's nothing besides this you want to talk about, get back to work."

Clearly he wasn't going to budge. "C'mon," I said. Once we were out of the room Oscar could no longer seal the flood gates as tears streamed down his face. "Stop crying, it's all good."

"I'm screwed!" he sobbed, voice shattering.

"Look, I told you we're gonna help you. We just have to do it on our own I guess."

"Yeah, bro, you gotta relax," Bari told him. Oscar's outburst surprisingly didn't invite attention from anyone. They all just continued working away in their cubicles like it hadn't even happened. But still, I wanted to get him back to our room before the wrong person noticed him.

"Lets just go work on your goggles." Why I said this without even knowing the science behind his invention is beyond me.

"I'm telling you, I tried everything, but every new thing I try to add screws it up," said Oscar.

"So you're just not gonna try to do anything about

what's happening to you?"

"I didn't say-"

"So lets go," I ordered, swatting his back much harder than intended.

Back at the room, Bari and I looked over Oscar's shoulder as he worked away on an invention. Just like I knew from the start, we weren't much help at all aside from providing words of encouragement to push him forward. But something was wrong. He abruptly stopped, tools in hand, yelling, "Damn!"

"What's up?" I asked.

"It's pointless." The defeat could clearly be heard in his voice, and before an attempt at swaying him could be made, Oscar flung his goggles at the wall like a dart, sending fragments of them flying on impact.

"Yo," Bari cried, running over to the mess, "we could've figured something out!"

"For what?" he asked. "So I can keep being their slave? Screw them!"

"Well now they're gonna kill you!"

"Not if we get them first." I said. "If we team up and get other workers in on this, we could stop them."

"Not happening," said Oscar.

"Why? I'm pretty sure a bunch of us could take a few old guys."

"Seems easy on paper, but I've tried it before and it's like everyone around here's brainwashed or something." His face lit up. "But, if you're serious, the three of us could get it done."

"Won't be enough," I replied skeptically. "And we're screwed if this doesn't work."

"You're screwed either way- all of us are," he said. "They use us and throw us away once they can't anymore. That's how it's always been. Enough's enough."

"I get that," I sighed, "but we can't even get through their shield. At least if we had more people, we could figure something out."

"That only causes more trouble; I'm telling you. And I've already got a plan."

Bari and I looked for him to expound.

"You said it yourself, it's a few old guys, right? And what if I told you there was a way through their shield too? Game over for them."

"I don't think it's that easy," said Bari.

"But it is," he said. "I can overload the power supply, and that should unlock their doors, screw up the security Striders interface, *and* weaken their shields enough to break through. Then we'll be able to hit them with everything we got. What're your inventions again?"

"Basically, electric pistols and grenades," I said simply.

"Perfect. So we doing this or not?"

I exchanged nods with Bari before we both jumped onboard.

△△△

Later on, we awaited Oscar a good distance from the throne room doors where two Striders stood guard. Since we had no way to communicate from afar, we agreed to meet up here at a designated time.

"You good?" asked Bari, disrupting my forward death stare.

"Just thinking," I said.

"Yo," called Oscar from behind us.

"We good?" I asked, turning to him.

"Yeah, I got the shield down, but we gotta hurry." Oscar now had a pistol in hand. I checked to ensure my EDP and ESG were ready as did Bari with his. "Lets go." We crashed through the throne room doors without the security Striders making a peep.

"Don't move!" I shouted. The two of us aimed at the 1st Echelon each with an EDP in one hand and an ESG ready in the other. Not one of their trio opened his mouth to make a smug remark; They all just sat there. But I didn't follow up my first order with anything, as I couldn't believe we'd gotten this far.

However, middle man eventually broke the silence asking, "Just what do you pests think you're doing?"

"Overthrowing you!" said Oscar with far more conviction than I thought was within him. "But I'm not letting that happen," he continued.

"What?" I said, turning around. Oscar, alongside the security Striders, pointed his pistol at me, then Bari, then back at me.

"What're you doing!?"

"Saving my life," he whispered.

"Think about it," I begged. "We got a chance to stop them and you're still gonna be their puppet?"

"What don't you understand? Nobody's stopping them and anyone's dead that tries. Sorry, but I'm with them."

The ringleader burst out laughing, almost choking between breaths. "Congratulations, Mr. Judes, you were right about them after all," he chuckled to his contemporaries. "You've earned yourself a promotion." I considered making a move to blast Oscar to oblivion for his betrayal. Even if he and the Striders blew me away first, Bari would have an opening for instant justice.

But before I could do a thing, middle man ordered the Striders to disarm and take us away. The Striders grabbed then pulled us to the exit while the three cowards proceeded to congratulate Oscar. We were left hopeless as both the throne room doors and our window of opportunity simultaneously slammed shut in our faces.

CHAPTER 16: PROPER INTRODUCTIONS

My hands begged me to slow down, but our situation demanded that I continue. The same Striders that escorted us to this lab on the buildings throne room floor two days prior now watched us constantly, guns at the ready, to ensure we put in the maximum amount of work. Although we got food throughout the day, leaving the floor was now off limits to us. Our captors said we would be under these conditions until further notice, but Bari's elaboration said they truly meant death the instant we maximized the potential of our creations. "I'm sorry, bro," I said, turning to Bari at my side.

"Don't start that, bro. We just gotta figure something else out," he whispered. But words of consolation meant nothing. This dire situation and missed opportunity to be half of what our dad was were both products of my blunders. "Let's just stall until-"

Out of nowhere, a zapping sound emerged and was directly followed by the smell of metal being burned.

When we spun around to investigate, the Striders monitoring us were sliced into pieces on the floor.

"What the heck?!" I said.

"Shut up before they hear you," scolded a familiar voice.

"Kayla?" asked Bari right before she, Pramin, Mu, and Rian appeared out of thin air.

"Hey," she said.

"What are you doing here!?" I asked. The four of them all had on exo armor and Pramin held his laser pointer.

"Change of plans, you're not giving yourselves up," said Kayla.

It's a little late for that, I thought. "Well where's Durai?"

"He told us wait here while he does something, but then some doors opened and we saw you guys," she replied.

"But I thought Durai said it was better to just do what they want," Bari pointed out.

"Yeah, but he changed his mind and we weren't just gonna let him come on his own." "Hey, where's everybody else at?" Mu spoke up.

"Yeah," added Rian, "I don't wanna be here any longer than we have to."

"They're here in cells."

"Like on this floor?" asked Kayla.

"Mhm."

"I guess those doors didn't open then, cause we didn't see them."

"Well we'll just have to make them open it for us."

"Is that so?" asked a new voice, causing us all to seek

out its owner who then appeared in the doorway. It was middle man. "You're not interfering with me!"

Kayla raised the EDP to shoot him but nothing happened when she pulled the trigger. The man then pulled out Durai's EMP, letting me know his true identity which was hidden underneath the Strider.

"The hell, Durai? Don't scare us like that," I said.

He remained silent, but one of his hands morphed into a gatling gun. "TEO is mine!" A stream of bullets came our way, sending us ducking for cover behind two adjacent tables until it abruptly ceased. "Give it up!"

"No!" Kayla barked back.

I grabbed an ESG from the table and tried to get it working to no avail. The EMP had momentarily disabled it.

"I won't ask you again!" said Durai.

After a bit more toying with it, the ESG lit up, so I quickly cranked the time knob before tossing it over at Durai. However, just as quickly as I threw it, it came flying back and landed beside me. I was immediately yanked up into the bubble where I could see blurred versions of everything outside of it.

"Get me down!" I cried, floating helplessly in the bubble.

"Lets not take this any further than its already gotten," suggested Durai. "Nobody needs to get hurt; just stay out of the way and let me finish this!"

Bari crawled over and closed the ESG, allowing gravity to pull me down onto the floor with a thud. "What's the matter with you!" I yelled from behind our cover.

"I'm not explaining a thing to you! Give up or die! Which is it?"

Silence rang throughout the room, but I refused to allow another cowardly traitor to screw us out of a prime opportunity. We now had the backup to take down the first Echelon, as well as save the others. My mind was made up, so I again set the ESG timer and tossed it, this time, quickly commanding Pramin to zap Durai with his laser. This diversion granted an opening for the ESG to successfully capture him.

"Stop! You don't know what you're doing!"

But his words meant nothing to me in that moment. All that mattered was finishing what I started. I stood up from behind the table, picked up an EDP charged it and fired. The instant contact was made with the bubble, sparks fused with pulses of energy to wildly overtake it. Every moment of this process caused Durai to yelp in agony as we all looked on. Kayla's face looked as if she wanted to intervene but the rest of her was frozen in place. Eventually, however, his blood curdling screams ceased as the bubble around him bursted in grand colorful fashion and Durai slammed face first on the floor. He layed motionless, smoke rising from his body.

Kayla was the first to run over and we all followed suit. Upon rolling him over, Durai's EMP was still clamped in the grasp of his hand while the Striders face was mostly cracked, revealing the person within. His beard was a dehydrated pattern of semi-grey patches, he had messy cornrows with follicles of hair sprouting from each braid, and his nose was semi wide from bridge to tip with a slight break just above the center.

Ivanna frowned. "Ugh, who's-"

"That's our dad," I replied, staring through him.

"So where's Durai? You guys knew about this?" she asked.

"No!" I snapped.

"Well we better get everybody else and leave while we still can," said Pramin.

"We're not going anywhere until we figure out what the hell's going on," I declared. "We're gonna make the 1st Echelon let everybody out and then they're gonna give us some answers."

No one was in disagreement.

"We're not just leaving him," said Bari.

Kayla checked his pulse. "He's breathing, but he's out."

"We'll come back for him," I assured right before a Strider entered the room.

"Stop! Or you'll be met with brute for-"

Bari and I simultaneously lit the android up using our EDP's alongside Pramin who joined in with his laser to make quick work of it.

"Lets go finish this," I said.

We walked out and down the hall toward the throne room which of course was locked. It was then that Kayla directed us to split up on either side of the entrance. "Burn a hole in it," she told Pramin.

He pulled out his laser and did just that, carving a large circle in the wall at which point, Kayla said, "Move in on three. One...two...three. She nudged the now weak part of the wall forward, and we charged in a line through the hole. I think we were all in agreement that trapping them for answers was far more valuable than simply killing them, but up on the throne platform, middle man was connected to his motionless counterparts by tubes, red with blood.

"Stop!" Kayla ordered, aiming at them. But she was paid no mind. "Hey, I said st-."

A patch of floor ahead of us slid open and the first thing to rise out were the hands and head of a Strider, pulling itself up. This wasn't your average Strider either. It stood tall at at least 8 feet and had extended blades for hands. That didn't stop Kayla from jumping straight into action though. She yelled for us all to spread out, swinging both hands above her head.

"Over here!" she egged the Strider on before dumping bullet after bullet into its head as it approached. She reeled back, narrowly dodging the first of three long swings. Bari and I both landed EDP shots that seemed to damage part of the Strider, but the laser softening up its back drew more attention. The blood-thirsty mech went right at Pramin who tripped over his own feet, trying to back up. Our combined flurry of fire from all angles, however, confused the Strider. It couldn't decide which of us to prioritize attacking. We, on the other hand, blasted away, doing a number on the Strider. Steady steps quickly turned weary and from there went limp. We were almost in the clear. At least that's what I thought before the floor once again opened, this time bringing forth three hounds of hell. Their mouths foamed in anticipation as the cage slowly opened. They stumbled over one another, rushing out at us.

Kayla downed one with her pistol right away while Pramin lasered another. But the third went right at me, and I panicked, missing my shot badly. It pounced on top of me and I blocked off my neck from its snapping jaw. I knew I couldn't hold him off for long, and just as my defense almost crumbled, a shot rang out. The hounds snarling attack turned to squeaky whimpers as it feel off of me, gasping for air. Kayla stood over the beast and put him out of his misery before helping me up.

"Watch it," Pramin cried out.

The Strider had mustered up one last attempt at our lives, but Kayla and I dodged the would-be impaling. We spread out like the others and kept unloading on the

Strider until it finally went down for the count, arm stiff in the air. Our attention reverted back to the 1st Echelon up on their throne platform where middle man then disconnected from his stiff comrades and stood up. His robe suddenly contorted outward in all directions until it's fabric gave way to a hulking monstrosity. While his height didn't change much, he made up for it in pumped up muscles. I squinted at his neck which still moved even after the transformation was complete. He had a face pulsating on each side of his throat, presumably the result of infusing his associates within himself.

"What a waste," he growled.

A peculiar odor suddenly found its way throughout

the room, dropping the others one-by-one until only middle man and I were left.

"What did you do to them?!" I yelled.

"Still standing huh? You've been taking your enhancement pills. Too bad they won't be enough to save you."

He leaped down from the platform with ease, landing in front of me, and my gadgets fell to the floor as he snatched my arm. I was thrown against the wall, and hardly gained my bearings when middle man speed walked towards me. His lunging swing just missed my head as I looped by him to grab my weapons. I fired a quick EDP shot to the head, but it only seemed to agitate him more as he chugged ahead. I stumbled over my feet, trying to backpedal and he yanked me up by the wrist, twisting it until my EDP again hit the floor. The ESG was choked up in my other hand until he lifted me both above his head and directly over the downed Striders blade. I glared down at it hopelessly before middle man went vertical, cocking me back on the way up, then forward as we descended. All I was focused on was avoiding impact. I fought it. I fought it as much as I could, but it wasn't enough to save me. The ESG, on the other hand, *was*. It sprung its bubble and caught us in mid-air, almost instantly slowing our momentum to a stop. I ended up on the bottom near the blade which stuck halfway into the bubble while middle man floated above. He could barely fit, let alone maneuver in the bubble. In fact, his broad shoulders hung on the outside, burning with each second. I soon felt his pain as well, shoving an arm through our enclosure. It singed my skin as I squirmed to reach the ESG below. Glancing up, I saw middle man struggle to reach me with an outstretched arm. I strained to reach further. More. More. This pain was the only alternative to death, so I kept pushing. More. More. I could feel middle man closing in, but his time was up. The ESG closed shut in my grasp, sending me to the floor and the skyward blade straight through his chest.

He roared in agony while I skidded away from his impaled body, tending to my wound.

"Everything alright?" someone called, climbing through our entry hole. It was Oscar, and he somehow recognized middle man, completely ignoring me to rush to his side. "How can I help?" he cried. But middle man could only groan in response. "I don't underst-

Middle man grabbed Oscar by the shoulder and reeled him in close, taking chomp after chomp at his throat before tossing him aside. This alone shook me to the core, but when he took it a step further, pushing himself off of the blade, I was scared stiff. He rattled his head to ignore the pain while limping towards me. But as he drew closer, the huffs and puffs slowed and got heavier. The wound was more than even *he* could handle. Middle man stumbled to his knees, letting out a final cry before falling face down, breathless. I thought he might be faking, so I sat there, staring at what I soon realized was his corpse before checking up on the others.

Thankfully, they were all still breathing and awoke

from their gas-induced sleep not long after. Everyone had questions that I was in no condition to answer when they saw the two dead bodies, so I brushed them all off for the time being. What mattered was that we were safe for the time being and could free the others which we went ahead and did.

Pramin burned gaping holes into each cell door for them to escape through. Molly along with Isaiah came from two of them while Ivanna was nowhere to be found.

"What're you guys doing here?" asked Molly.

"We thought you could use a hand," replied Kayla.

Molly warmly embraced her. "Thank you."

Isaiah was too busy kneeling, giving praise to The Most High to say anything to us just yet.

"Ivanna?" I called, peeking into her cell, only to see her on her knees, hands together, facing the wall.

"Ivanna," I said again, causing her to spring up and face me with lit up eyes. I suppose her prayer had been answered as she then ran over and, to my surprise, pressed her subtlely glossy lips against mine. Not knowing how to reply, I smiled asking the others what we were going to do now while Ivanna got down to join her dad.

"Where's Durai?" asked Molly.

"We don't know," Bari told her. "But somehow our dad's here right now. None of this makes any sense." The shattering of his voice as he spoke made it clear Bari was nearly brought to tears.

"To hell with it," she mumbled. "You're father never died and there's no such person as Durai Garvish."

"What are you saying?"

"Ever since your dad finished his masterpiece, he had a chip on his shoulder cause the 1st Echelon didn't promote him. He gave them their biggest cash cow, and they just kept him at a low level position. When he first signed his contract, he was hoping to reach a high enough level to see what they had planned and stop them so he could take over, but it didn't work out that way."

"So-"

"So then he got them to help fake his and his wives deaths. He gave them some B.S excuse, but he really did it to keep you two out of all this and stop the 1st Echelon."

"But why'd he try to kill us!?" I asked. "If he wanted to protect us, why ask for our help and then shoot at us?"

"He was obsessed," she said. "All that mattered was finishing what he started, especially after the strings he had to pull. TEO didn't even know about Accessible Striders or that he and his wife lived double lives for years with them. He was Durai. She was Molly."

I instantly realized the implication of this statement, but before I could react, Molly stripped down before the two halves of her body opened like doors, revealing my mother who then stepped out of the Strider. Her hair was straightened, flowing down her back, and she wore white shorts, an orange shirt, and polka-dot socks.

Bari looked at our mother in amazement which annoyed me. I wanted him to be as pissed off as me given everything we'd been put through for the sake of our dad's pride.

"Look, I know you're upset with us, Naaji, but now's not the time to go back and forth," she said. "We need to get your father and get out of here."

By some miracle, I had enough composure to keep calm, but it became more and more frail with each step back where we'd left my father whose eyes now flickered about. "Aye," I nudged him roughly.

My mother dove to his side. "Stop it," she cried.

But I didn't care. I just wanted answers. "You could've just told us, you know."

He murmured something.

"What?!"

"My legs," he groaned. "I can't feel my legs."

"Who's fault is that?" I scolded. "You could've just told us what was going on and none of this would've happened."

"I couldn't."

"Why not," I huffed.

He thought about his next reply momentarily. "I did what was best for all of us."

"Bullshit!"

"You're not helping, Naaji!" said my mom, tending to him.

"*I'm* not helping? Both of you let us think you were dead, and now I'm just supposed to shut up and be happy you faked the whole thing?"

"That's not what I said."

"That's what it sounds like. And it's crazy to me how you're defending the one that was cheating on you."

The instant I said this, I regretted it as my mother's

spirit was crushed before me. She hopelessly looked to my dad who didn't offer a word in response before the doors flew open behind us, sending her flying to her feet.

"Watch out!" she pointed.

A burst of bullets whizzed by, and I heard a thud before we all exchanged blasts with the lone Strider. It shot wildly, unsure who to lock in on. The shootout quickly came to an end, but not before three bodies were made limp at my feet.

Mustapha. Pramin. Ivanna. All downed by the Strider. But not only them. The first thud was my mother's body which laid draped in blood over my father. For what felt like an eternity, everyone but myself and Isaiah were too shaken to move as he tried helping Ivanna, and I, my mother.

"Why father!?" he cried to the ceiling.

He got no answer, and neither did I, supporting my mother's pierced head with both hands. The others finally snapped out of it and tried to aid our fallen, but it was no use, and while the shots still rang in my ears, I

faintly heard my father call my name. Resting her head on him, I leaned in closer.

"It's because of this." I waited for him to elaborate. "This is why I couldn't tell you. This life comes with too much shit to get anyone you care about mixed up with. I didn't even want your mother to know, but I couldn't do it alone," he said.

"Well we finished it. First Echelon's dead, and now so are they," I pointed. "You happy now?"

"It's not finished at all. Don't forget, this is only one of their headquarters and one set of leaders."

"Then we'll get rid of the rest of them," I said.

"That's the only option, but there's no reason to put anyone else in danger. You and me can finish what I started," he said.

I turned to the others who were still hopelessly clinging to the dead. Though these were the last things I wanted to see and hear, he was right. But there still lied an obvious problem.

"They'll never go for that," I whispered.

"Of course not," he replied, activating his EMP. "Make them." He gave me the pistol from his side, and I hesitantly turned to the others. But the glimpse I caught of Ivanna's lifeless body in her father's arms made up my mind.

"Hey!" I yelled, getting their attention. "You gotta go."

"What!?" Kayla contested.

I raised the gun. "Leave! We'll handle the rest of this." She tried to pull a fast one and blast me with the EDP but it was already out of commission. "Go!" I snapped, springing Isaiah to his feet.

"Naaji," he said, "what're you doing?"

I already knew what he wanted: he'd try defuse the situation and lecture me into submitting the gun. But I refused to let anyone change my mind, and Bari knew it. His tear-drained eyes wouldn't leave me for an instant as he whimpered, unable to get a word out.

"Get out!" I cried. "Just drop all the stuff and get outta here!"

They finally understood I meant business and obeyed as I escorted them back to the elevator, never letting up my aim. Of course they tried to reason with me, but I was far past that. No one else I cared for, especially Bari, would be in harm's way any longer. As his mouth finally jumped open to speak, the doors closed between us.

EPILOGUE: ONE WEEK LATER

I entered the lab as my father was hunched over his desk, hard at work. "Here," I said, placing a bottle of his favorite soda.

He didn't look up, but thanked me.

"Sure you don't need any more help?"

"I'll let you know; I'm good for now."

As I turned to take a walk, my foot nipped the side of his wheelchair, but he said nothing, so neither did I.

Once in the hall, I couldn't help but shutter as I passed the chamber where we'd power washed and stored the bodies for the time being. I'd never been as engrossed in anything like I was in our new conquest after separating from the others, with whom we hadn't been in contact with since. This was not for a lack of trying though: on at least three occasions they tried to confront us, only to be escorted from the lobby by security striders we'd programmed to do so. Being stripped of all gadgets certainly didn't help their cause either, and while they couldn't understand why we did what we did, I knew it was best for us -no- best for all.

www.ingramcontent.com/pod-product-compliance
Lightning Source LLC
Chambersburg PA
CBHW050939120626
46552CB00001B/279